Abigail's Mirror

Book 2

Melissa Strangway

iUniverse, Inc.

New York   Bloomington

Abigail's Mirror

This is a work of fiction. All of the characters, names, incidents,
organizations, and dialogue in this novel are either the products
of the author's imagination or are used fictitiously.

iUniverse books may be ordered through booksellers or by contacting:

iUniverse
1663 Liberty Drive
Bloomington, IN 47403
www.iuniverse.com
1-800-Authors (1-800-288-4677)

Because of the dynamic nature of the Internet, any Web addresses or
links contained in this book may have changed since publication and
may no longer be valid. The views expressed in this work are solely those
of the author and do not necessarily reflect the views of the publisher,
and the publisher hereby disclaims any responsibility for them.

ISBN: 978-1-4401-6176-6 (pbk)
ISBN: 978-1-4401-6175-9 (ebk)

Printed in the United States of America

iUniverse rev. date: 1/5/2010

Chapter 1

Ravine waited at the bottom step, running her fingers along the rusted railing. She stood on her tiptoes to peer into the store, watching a handful of customers through the large front window. This place never had more than a few browsers at any time, and she watched as they picked up trinkets and other old junk, turning the pieces once or twice before placing them back on the shelves. As usual, these shoppers looked around to be sure no one was watching as they discreetly wiped their hands.

The rotted and splintered wood of the shutters hung on either side of the door like sharpened daggers, and the faded blue paint on the siding blistered from years of morning sun and no fresh paint. Even today's clear sky and uncommonly warm weather failed to brighten the look of the store. With November just around the corner, she thought, all the rest of the street would soon be drab as well, so this place wouldn't stand out like such an open sore.

Her own reflection was dull in the smudged and dirty glass. But she adjusted her ball cap, pushed her glasses higher up on her nose, and started up the steps. The rickety wood beneath her sneakers creaked and groaned. Stopping half way, she could already see through the window the disappointed expressions of the shoppers.

Grabbing tightly on the railing, Ravine headed for the front door.

Above her head, a big sign hung dangerously from one good hinge and another that someone had tried to string together with wire. It swung in the slight breeze, banging loudly against the weathered siding. *Maybe Antiques*, the sign read. As it swayed unsteadily over her head, she hoped no one would be underneath it when the wind finally brought it down some day.

Suddenly the door flew open, and two women swept past Ravine as if she weren't there, carelessly pushing her up against the railing.

"Well, Agatha, that was a huge waste of our time, don't you think?"

"Yes, it was. It was most certainly not like the antique shop we saw earlier. This was just a collection of rubbish."

As they quickly headed down the steps, Ravine heard the second woman continue, "Why, Hildy, did you buy that piece of junk, anyway? What on earth are you going to do with it?"

A disgusted sneer crossed over Hildy's face. Then, at the bottom of the steps, she took the brown bag containing her pity purchase, and threw it into the garbage bin at the curb.

"That's what," she said. "That's where it belongs."

Ravine heard them laugh as they hurried away, and she stuck out her tongue, even though she knew they couldn't see her.

A bell tinkled as Ravine opened the door, and she stood on the threshold looking in. The clutter of *Maybe Antiques* always fascinated her. There was stuff everywhere. Trinkets were scattered across desktops, coffee tables, and shelves. Bigger items littered the floor and added to the chaos and confusion. The aisles were narrow and laid out like a maze, almost as if designed by accident. Some of the big floor items were packed so close together that there had to be little paths between them. Here and there were little alcoves, and a couple of side-rooms that led off the main area. They were full of more stuff, and an old treasure chest full of tattered and dusty old books sat in the middle of one of these rooms.

This place had been here since long before Ravine was born, and even though she had been in and out of it a few times long ago with her mother, it was only in the past year or so that she had started coming here a lot on her own. She had made friends with the owner.

"Good morning, my dear," said Onna. Golden bracelets, on both arms, clanged against each other as she waved to Ravine.

Ravine smiled when she saw the bright red ribbon in Onna's hair and the diamond studded glasses balancing on the tip of her nose. Today, her silver hair hung loose to her waist. The diamonds weren't real, and neither were the stones in the matching rings Onna wore on every finger. She was wearing the same outfit she had on when Ravine visited last Saturday, and she looked grand.

"Hi, Onna."

Onna's sapphire eyes sparkled when she smiled, a smile that lit up her face and chased away the wrinkles.

Onna was known to everyone as Oliver Owen's wife. Even though he was gone now, people still called her Ollie's wife. This was Ollie's store, and

Onna had only kept it open this past year to keep her memories of him near.

'Honestly, woman,' Ravine remembered hearing him say, 'you care more about gossiping than you do about the business!'

Ravine guessed that probably wasn't true, but she knew Onna only worked in the store before Oliver died because it made him happy. Onna told her one day how out of place she felt amongst the antiques and collectables. But almost everyone else, Ravine knew, would think of Onna as a walking billboard for the store because she looked like an antique herself.

Ravine understood. She knew how it was like to feel like you didn't quite fit.

Onna did her best now that she was on her own to take care of the shop. But she didn't have a head for business, nor a mind for sales. When Oliver was alive, her only job was to count the cash, which she got wrong every time. Oliver would always step in to balance the sale.

Before Oliver's death, the store was called *Small Antiques*. But after he was gone, Onna made a new sign by scratching out 'Small' and painting the word 'Maybe' over top. Everyone understood that Ollie had the eye for antiques, and she knew she couldn't fool anyone. Gradually, people began to use the shop as a place to drop off their junk. Onna never refused any donation, and *Maybe Antiques* turned quickly into a disorganized mess.

"Anything new today?" Ravine asked, poking around the dusty selves. She wiped her hands on her jeans.

"Only that mirror, dear," Onna said, her eyes twinkling.

Ravine glanced in the direction Onna was pointing.

The mirror was leaning against the wall of death. Well, that was Ravine's name for it, anyway. The red paint on the wall looked like blood, oozing through the cracks of the aging wood.

The mirror was a heavy old thing, a little taller than Ravine. It had a beautiful, but aged, wooden frame with a hand-carved angel on its top. Although it hadn't been in the store last Saturday, it had already gathered a *Maybe Antiques* layer of dust.

Even when the sun was shining outside, it was always dim inside the store. But today, as the sun peeked through the small window above the book alcove, the dust sparkled. Ravine thought the dust dancing in the sunlight made the mirror look magical.

"Where did the mirror come from?" she asked. Standing close to it, she felt a coldness fall upon her.

She rubbed her arms and glanced at Onna, who didn't seem to notice the sudden icy air around them.

"Mr. Baldwin dropped it off," she began. "You know Mr. Baldwin, don't you? He owns the pastry shop around the corner. Oh, Ollie used to love his scones. Every morning he'd say to me 'Dear, run over and get me some of those things that I like over there.' I always knew what he was talking about, so I would --"

"The mirror, Onna. What about the mirror?"

"Oh yes, the mirror. Well, it's a strange story, I'd say. Mr. Baldwin says no one in the family knows where the mirror came from. After Mrs. Baldwin passed away, that's his mother, not his wife, because you know, dear, Mr. Baldwin's wife never took his last name. I don't know why women do that these days. They get married and don't change their names. I was honored to take Oliver's last name. Owen, that's a very strong name you know."

Onna took a breath and gazed at her reflection. She straightened out her purple sequined sweater and ran her fingers through her hair. Her rings reflected off the glass, creating an image that reminded Ravine of the bright lights on a Ferris wheel.

"What were we talking about again, dear?"

"The mirror." At this rate, it was going to take all day for her to find out anything about the mirror, Ravine thought.

"Oh yes, the mirror. Well, after Mrs. Baldwin died, that's his mother now, the family auctioned everything off. You know, at the old auction building down on Superior Road. The big silver building. You can't miss it. I always think it looks like a great big soup can with the label peeled off. You know, I would imagine it gets really hot inside there in the summer --"

"Onna, please!"

"Yes, of course, dear," Onna sniffed. "Well, Mr. Baldwin told me that when the auction was all done, they went in to lock up the house. They aren't sure what they're going to do with the old place, you know. But they found this mirror sitting inside an open closet. It was the strangest thing, he said. The mirror just showed up out of nowhere. No one knows how it got in the house, and no one could recall ever seeing it before. Mr. Baldwin had a copy of the auction list, but the mirror wasn't on the list neither. Everybody was so sure it just wasn't there before the auction. So, instead of taking it back to the auctioneer, they brought it here."

"But how can a mirror just show up? Things just don't appear out of nowhere," Ravine said.

"That's exactly what I'm saying. And I told Mr. Baldwin that. I said 'things just don't appear out of thin air', but he assured me that this one did. The mirror appeared out of nowhere, he said."

Onna paused.

"I really think that someone just forgot to put the mirror on the auction list, and no one wanted to admit they missed something this big."

Ravine and Onna stared at their dusty reflections for a moment. Ravine watched as Onna went back to her seat behind the counter and started to pat Timmy. He rolled on to his back, stretched in a sunbeam, and began to purr.

Ravine continued to look around the store.

Maybe Antiques was full of clocks. Most of them worked, but only one actually showed the correct time. It was the big grandfather clock that stood in front of the wall of death, right beside where Onna had placed the mirror. Ravine was suddenly reminded of the one accurate clock, when it began to chime loudly, five times, and startled her into realizing she was already late for supper.

"I gotta go," Ravine said. "My mom is probably already pacing the living room wondering where I am." She quickly headed toward the door and added, "I promised her I wouldn't be late." She slipped out as a few more customers came in.

"Bye, Onna," she yelled as she ran down the stairs. She stopped just long enough to clean the dust from her glasses, and then hurried home. Even running as fast as she could, she was still going to be in trouble.

She opened the door and walked into an empty living room. As her heart slowed to a normal pace, the clock over the fireplace showed it was already quarter past five. So she went to kitchen for the lecture she knew she was going to get.

The table was set and ready, but no one was seated. Her mom stood near the counter with the phone cradled on her shoulder, talking softly. She lifted supper out of the oven, smiling at Ravine as she placed the steaming dish on the table. A few more words were said into the phone, and then she hung up.

"Hi, honey. Just in time," her mom said. She threw her oven mitts on the counter. "Dad will be a few minutes late. He got called into the office today."

"On a Saturday?"

"Yes, on a Saturday. This is the third weekend in a row," her mother sighed.

Ravine sat at the table as her mom fiddled at the counter. So where's the responsibility lecture, she wondered. Last summer, if she had been just five minutes late, she would have had to endure the speech. Maybe even from both parents.

While she watched her mother getting things ready, Ravine thought how things had changed over the past year. Life in the Crawl house was finally getting back to normal. Sure, they all thought about Rachel and visited her grave frequently. But, slowly, things were changing.

Her mother was busy again. Ravine was never really sure what her mother was busy with, but things felt the same as they did before her sister died. Mostly, it meant that her mother was giving her a little more space, instead of constantly worrying where Ravine was or what she was doing.

Her mother was even experimenting in the kitchen again. She had always loved gourmet cooking, and now she was at it again. Ravine liked that too, because her mom botched most of the recipes, and they often needed to be rescued by the pizza delivery guy. Ravine didn't see any problem there. Pizza was never a bad idea.

"So what did you and Derek do this afternoon?"

The front door opened and slammed shut.

"Oh, he was at his grandma's today, so I just hung out with Joannie," Ravine fibbed. Her mother didn't like *Maybe Antiques* and she didn't want to get into an argument. She tried not to look at her mother as she helped set the table, just in case her mom could see the fib on her face.

"Linda, sometimes I wonder why I even have employees," her father growled, as he came into the kitchen and sat down. He didn't look happy.

"Do you know why they called me in? Because they didn't know how to work the new fax machine," he added, without waiting for an answer.

Ravine's mom listened with her elbows on the table and her chin resting on the back of her hands. This was her 'listening to Robbie's long speech about work' position.

"Did you get it figured out for them?"

"No. I gave them a book. The one that came with the fax machine. It's called *How to Use Your New Fax Machine*. I told them it probably wasn't a real good sign that the book was still wrapped in plastic. Then I left."

As he started helping himself to supper, he smiled at Ravine.

"Hi. How was your day? Hang out with Derek?" he asked.

"He's at his grandma's."

While her parents chatted, Ravine coasted in and out of the conversation. And her thoughts wandered back to the mirror in Onna's shop. It was a weird looking thing, but beautiful all the same, she thought.

As her parents continued to talk, she carefully lined up the green beans on her plate like little soldiers, separating them from the enemy carrots with a pile of mashed potatoes. As her fork made tracks in the potatoes, she wondered if the carrots and beans could see each other behind the potato barricade.

Then she had an odd thought. When she was looking into the mirror in Onna's shop, something had seemed a little off, but she had no idea what. When you look into a mirror, it's always you looking back. But thinking about it now, she wasn't sure if it had felt like it was only her looking back. And there was that sudden feeling of cold.

She shook her head. This is nuts, she thought. Of course it was me looking back at me in the mirror.

And of course the beans and carrots can see each other.

After dinner, Ravine helped clean up and then waited for her parents on the front verandah. Finally, they all piled into the car and drove down the wide street, heading to Summerhill Drive.

It wasn't a long trip, and even with her eyes closed Ravine knew each winding turn and stop.

They had been here many times. And Ravine had been here often without her parents.

Her dad parked the car outside the gates of Summerhill Cemetery. This late in October, it was getting dark early, so they would only have a few minutes before the cemetery closed for the night.

They got out of the car and all three doors seemed to slam shut in unison. The iron gates loomed over them in the dim light. From here, towering monuments to the west, looking like dark sentries, watched over the smaller gravestones, guarding them until the morning light. But the Crawls headed up the path in the other direction, toward the older part of the cemetery.

Ravine slowed once in a while, brushing her hand over century-old inscriptions. Dates and names of people from long ago. Some of these graves were almost hidden under overgrown shrubs, and most of the stones were cracked and slowly decaying. She wondered why nobody came to look after them. Wasn't there any family to remember these people?

By now, Ravine was walking quite a few paces behind her parents. She stopped beside a gravestone and touched the familiar name carved in it: Isabel Roberts. She felt a lump in her throat. No, Isabel, I will never forget you.

Ravine continued on, touching the names and whispering the dates under her breath. Suddenly, she thought she felt a zap of electricity shoot through her fingers as she touched a small stone. She jerked her hand away, but a chill swept over her as she cautiously reached out to touch it again.

In the cool autumn air, the stone felt warm under her fingertips. She knelt down. Abigail Baldwin. Her spine tingled. She remembered this grave. It was one that she and Derek had talked about during the summer when they visited the cemetery in search of answers about Isabel. One of them had commented that there was a Baldwin family that lived on the street next to theirs, and they wondered if it might be the same family.

And then today she saw this beautiful mirror that came from a Baldwin family. That's a lot of coincidence, she thought.

She stood up just as a sudden gust of wind howled in her ear. She zipped up her jacket, pulling it closer to her. Her head began to throb. This was not the first time Ravine had experienced something like this.

"Are you coming?" her mother called. She was heading back toward Ravine, seemingly unaffected by the chill or the sudden wind.

Ravine backed away from the gravesite.

"Yes, Mom … I'm coming."

She hurried away from Abigail's grave, running to catch up to her parents.

Ravine drew in a breath. The fragrance of the fall chrysanthemums reminded Ravine of the way Rachel used to smell before she became sick. The mums had spread quickly over the past year, and the two shrubs she had planted were now about three feet high. Rachel's grave was well maintained.

The Crawls stood in silence. There were no words needed. Ravine's father had his arm around her mother's shoulder, and Ravine was squeezed in between, holding her mother's hand.

After a short while, they simply turned and left, heading back down the hill to the car. As they went, Ravine felt another gust of wind pick up around her. A howling sound whipped by her head. She looked at her parents, but they didn't seem to notice.

Then, just as they reached the gates, she thought she could hear a voice crying out behind her. Ravine stopped and turned around, but no one was there. She hurried to the car, but she was sure she could still hear crying and whimpering behind her.

"Honey, are you okay?" her mother asked. "Do you have a headache?"

Ravine realized neither of them could hear the cries. She shuddered.

"It's okay, Mom, I'm fine," she said as they reached the car.

"I know it doesn't get easier, sweetheart," her dad began. "If you don't want to come next week, I understand."

"No, Dad. Really, I'm fine." Ravine opened the car door.

The ringing in Ravine's ears didn't stop until they were just a block from home. And by the time they pulled into the driveway, she really did have a headache. That was the perfect excuse to lock herself in her room for the rest of the night. But as she climbed the stairs to her room, she realized she really was tired.

She got into her pajamas and crawled into bed. Clean sheets, she thought. Cool and crisp. Mom must have changed the linen today. It took a few minutes for her to feel warm.

As Ravine closed her eyes, she could hear the cries in her head once more. This time, it was more like a whimper.

Then she heard Onna's words in her head. "That's exactly what I'm saying. And I told Mr.

Baldwin that. I said 'things just don't appear out of thin air', but he assured me that this one did."

Ravine fell into a restless sleep. Hazy images of *Maybe Antiques* and that weird mirror filled her head. The whimpering sound became louder as the mirror came into focus. Ravine was standing in front of it, looking. But the blurry image looking back wasn't her.

Sunday morning was grey and cloudy. Ravine woke with a dull pain still inside her head. And she could remember her dreams vividly.

Rolling over, she thought about the mirror in Onna's shop. And the more she thought about it, the sharper the pain in her head became.

She needed to go back to see the mirror. She thought about calling Derek to see if he wanted to go with her, but decided against it. Something told her she should go alone.

Ravine dressed quickly, in her best ripped jeans and her most faded pink t-shirt. As she started downstairs, she could hear her parents in the kitchen. Halfway down the stairs, she yelled.

"I'm going out! I'll be back later!"

Her mother was waiting for her in the hallway.

"Don't you want any breakfast, sweetheart?"

"No, Mom. I'm not really hungry this morning." Actually, she was famished.

"How's your headache?" her father asked. He looked out from the kitchen, holding his coffee in one hand and his newspaper in the other. Ravine could never figure out how he could hold up an open newspaper with one hand.

"Good. Good. Much better!" The pounding in her head continued.

"It's a little cooler today, sweetheart, so take your jacket."

"No, I'll be okay."

She opened the front door and ran down the steps. Almost immediately, she realized she should have brought her jacket, but she didn't want to waste time going back to get it.

It took a little longer to get to Onna's, because she wasn't running. Without looking, she walked up the stairs and grabbed the doorknob. It was locked.

Oh no, she thought. I forgot Onna told me she was never going to open on Sunday anymore.

She stared in through the window, hoping if Onna were around that she would be let in. She could see Timmy snoozing on the counter, but there was no sign of Onna. She tried knocking, but all she managed to do was make Timmy yawn and roll over.

"Oh, I'm going to start closing on Sundays, dear," Onna had told her. "I don't know why I ever started opening. Just to keep myself busy, I guess. Ollie was never open on Sundays. He always said it was a day to rest. If God rested on Sunday, then we should rest on Sunday. Ollie would roll over in his grave if he knew I was opening on Sunday mornings."

Ravine left the shop, still thinking about the mirror, and headed back to Water Street. She crossed the road to avoid the construction site, and headed up Derek's front lawn. She rang the bell and it was a few minutes before his mother answered.

"Hi Ravine. Derek's not here, he's over at Sunil's."

Walking home, Ravine thought about calling Joannie or Lisa. But something about yesterday's trip to the cemetery was bugging her.

Even though it was cooler, the sun had at last come out and it was a gorgeous day. Ravine decided to get her bike. On a day like today, it wouldn't take long to get to the cemetery.

It was a crisp ride, and she regretted again that she hadn't brought her jacket. But she rode easily through the winding roads and up the hills. She hopped off her bike at the gates and propped it up against a tree.

This time she wasn't going to visit her sister's grave. It was Abigail's she wanted.

As she approached, the wind picked up again, just as it had yesterday.

"Abigail Baldwin," she whispered as she touched the stone. And like yesterday, she could feel a tingle from the stone, like a small electric shock. It felt warm to the touch.

"Abigail Baldwin," she whispered again.

Then as the dull ache began in her head, the wind picked up again.

"1872-1882," Ravine said, out loud.

A couple of months earlier, when she and Derek were here looking for information about Isabel, this grave only caught their attention because of the short life of this girl. She was ten years-old, about the same the same age as them when she died.

Derek and Ravine's birthdays were only three days apart. Last month they turned eleven, and when they had their little private birthday ceremony, Derek had joked that at least they had outlived Abigail Baldwin.

But today the cemetery felt different. The sudden rising breeze, the voice she heard on the wind yesterday, hearing the Baldwin name repeatedly, made her wonder. What was drawing her to Abigail Baldwin?

Ravine stood up and left the graveyard. This time, the wind and the voice didn't follow her.

Chapter 2

"I saw this great mirror at *Maybe Antiques*, and I thought after school you could come and get it with me. I might need some help carrying it home."

Derek and Ravine walked against the wind. Derek had slept in, and now they were hurrying toward the schoolyard as the bell rang.

"I can't today. Sunil and I have a basketball match," Derek said.

The bell rang again and they hurried into the yard.

"Cancel. This is more important," Ravine replied. They headed to the back of the slow moving line.

"I doubt it. I can't see how buying some mirror is more important than playing basketball."

Inside the school, the hallway was congested with shoes, coats, backpacks and loud children going every which way. A younger girl hurrying off to class apologized for bumping into Ravine, but Ravine didn't notice the bump, and didn't hear the apology.

"I have a feeling this mirror is special," Ravine said quietly, waiting for a reaction from Derek. When one didn't come, she tried again. "You know what I mean."

Derek grabbed his binders. "Yeah, I know what you mean. I'd rather hang out with Sunil and play basketball."

Ravine watched as Derek headed into the classroom without her. She followed him and plopped down in her seat, just behind him. Her math book hit the desk with a heavy thud.

"Okay, how about tomorrow then?"

Derek turned around and leaned as close as he could.

"I don't want anymore adventures like this summer. I just want to hang out with our friends and be normal," he whispered. "I've told you that before, Ravine."

Before Ravine could comment, Mrs. MacDonald started to speak.

The morning was a blur for Ravine. Whatever the teacher was saying, Ravine didn't hear any of it. It wasn't like Derek to be so short with her. He was always willing to help her with anything. It was always her and Derek doing things together; but she had noticed this past week he was keeping his distance. Yeah, he had told her that he just wanted to be normal. And he had said that all during the time they were helping Isabel and solving her mystery too. But he still helped when he was needed, so she figured he would be interested if there was something else weird going on.

Derek wasn't listening to Mrs. MacDonald either, but it didn't have anything to do with Ravine or her new mystery. He really did just want to be a normal kid, and he hoped whatever had made it possible for him to talk to ghosts during the summer had gone away.

But it wasn't that.

His mind raced through the sequence of events this morning. Something strange was going on with his mother.

When he had come into the kitchen for breakfast, she was talking on the phone. She stopped as soon as she saw him, and then started up again. But it seemed to him that she had changed the conversation, almost like he had walked in and caught her at something.

And this morning wasn't the first time. Last week, when he got home from school, he stood in the hallway for a while, listening to his mother. He could tell she was on the phone, and it was obvious she was upset.

"Why now? You can't be serious," he remembered her saying. "This is a lot to dump on me all at once. Besides, you should ask him instead of me. He's a good boy. He'll know what's right for him."

When Derek entered the kitchen, his mother became silent. Then she abruptly ended the call. He asked her about it, but she said she was not talking about him. He was pretty sure that wasn't true.

All that evening, Derek was quite certain his mother kept stealing glances at him, almost as if she didn't want him to know she was looking at him. Strange glances. Sad glances.

He was going to mention it to Ravine, but he wasn't sure what to say. There was probably nothing to worry about, and Ravine would make a big deal out of nothing. No, it was better to keep this to himself for now.

At the end of the day, Derek and Sunil threw their packs on the ground by the basketball court. As Derek started warming up, he saw Ravine walk by. He felt a twinge of regret with how he treated her earlier.

"Come shoot some hoops with us!"

Ravine kept walking and, without looking at him, she yelled, "I'm going to *Maybe Antiques*."

Sunil bounced the ball between his legs. "That's weird Ravine doesn't want to play," he commented. "Why is she going to the junk store?"

Derek just shrugged. "Her loss," he said.

Sunil stared at him, surprised.

As Ravine climbed the rickety steps, the sign still banged loudly against the wooden siding. There was a long crack in the front window and Ravine guessed Onna did not have the money to replace it.

She opened the door and the bell jingled above her head. Ravine looked around. The shop appeared to be empty, except for Timmy, who was lying on a shelf where he had found the last sunbeam of the afternoon.

But the mirror was still there, and she walked over to the wall of death where it was leaning. That's funny, she thought. Onna has cleaned it. And dusted it. Onna never dusts anything.

As Ravine approached the mirror, it was suddenly cold. Just like before. She reached out to touch the mirror, but this time her fingers tingled only slightly. She ran her fingers along the frame, feeling the detailed carving in the wood. She hadn't noticed yesterday how fancy the frame was. The angel on top was polished and shiny, but the carvings along the sides of the frame were blackened with age and dirt. She thought it was probably leaves and petals.

"Ah, my dear, you're back!"

Ravine jumped, startled. She turned to see Onna coming from the back of the store.

"Couldn't stay away?"

"There's just something about this mirror," Ravine began.

"Well, my dear, you are not the only one who has shown an interest in it," Onna said. "A couple came in today and were looking at it. Nice couple. An older couple. Not as old as me, mind you, but old still the same. Some days I feel like there isn't anybody as old as me. It looked as if the man was younger than the woman. A lot younger, too. I'd say maybe about ten years younger or so. Handsome fella, too. It's a wonder he was with someone so much older than himself."

"They liked the mirror?"

"Oh my, did they ever! They even had me wipe it off so they could take a better look at it. They were here for half an hour, admiring it. Then, when they were ready to buy it, she changed her mind. Just like that." Onna snapped her fingers. "It was quite strange, to say the least. They went on and on about it, and then she turns toward the mirror and this terrible expression crosses her face and she grabs the man's hand and whisks him out of here."

Ravine stared at their reflections in the mirror. Onna looked tired today. Her hair was tousled, and she had dark circles under her eyes. Ravine's own cheeks were red from the cool autumn wind, and her glasses had slipped down her nose. She pushed them back up.

The bell rang, and Onna hurried off to see her new customers.

As Ravine was about to turn away from the mirror, she thought she saw it glow. Just a little. A soft round glow like a flashlight that was very far off, almost too far away to see. Then it seemed to brighten a little. She looked behind her to see where the light was coming from, but just then the grandfather clock reminded her she was going to be late again.

Onna was busy with her customers, so Ravine quickly slipped out without saying goodbye.

All the way home she thought about the mirror. Maybe Derek would want to come here with her tomorrow. She wanted to know if he would feel the cold or see the light.

When Derek got home, he wasn't surprised to find his mother on the phone again. Like the last few times, she became silent and abruptly ended the call.

"Who was on the phone?" he asked, throwing down his backpack in the middle of the kitchen floor.

He opened the fridge door, analyzing the contents inside. Unimpressed, he shut the door and sat down.

"So who was on the phone?" he asked again.

"No one important. Just business. Take your backpack upstairs and start on your homework until supper."

Derek stood up and opened the fridge again. "I'm hungry," he complained.

"Well, it's all the same stuff in there that was in there a few minutes ago," she said, nodding toward the fridge.

Derek slammed the door and grabbed his things off the floor as the phone rang again. He went to reach for the receiver.

"I've got it," his mother said, shooing him out.

Derek rushed upstairs to his mother's room. Her phone was sitting on her bedside table. He walked toward it and sat on the bed. Gently, he lifted the receiver with his finger still on the button. Then gradually he removed his finger hoping his mother wouldn't hear a click.

"Give me some time to think about this," she was saying. "I haven't even mentioned it to Derek yet."

"But you do agree, don't you?"

"You have sprung this on me quite suddenly. I will call you when I have a chance to sort all this out myself, and then I need to find a way to approach Derek. You make this sound so simple, but it's not."

"I understand. Call me after you have had more time to think about it. Then maybe I can talk to Derek."

The phone went dead. Derek replaced the receiver, his heart pounding. He quickly went to his room, shutting the door behind him all the time wondering who his mother was talking to and what it had to do with him. It wasn't a voice he recognized.

Ravine couldn't keep her mind off the mirror all week. She asked Derek on Tuesday and Wednesday if he would go to *Maybe Antiques*, but he was grumpy and turned her down. She noticed it wasn't just her he was being strange with. Sunil wanted to shoot hoops with him, but Derek said he needed to go home. Derek never passed up a chance to play basketball.

Ravine went to Onna's every day after school to make sure the mirror was still there. She knew she wouldn't be able to purchase it until the weekend when she might be able to get it home and sneak it up to her bedroom. There would still be questions, especially when her mother found out she got it from Onna's shop. Ravine knew she would be in for a lecture about wasting her allowance on junk at *Maybe Antiques*.

On Thursday, she was looking at the mirror when Onna came up behind her.

"It sure is a special mirror, my dear."

Ravine nodded.

"It's really a work of art," Onna said.

Ravine nodded again. She reached out to wipe off a little speck of dust, and an electric shock zapped through her fingers. She pulled away quickly as her pulse quickened.

"I haven't seen a mirror like this since I was a little girl," Onna continued. "My grandmother used to have one. Not exactly the same, though, because there was no little angel on top. Oh, I remember spending the summer at my grandmother's place. She had this big old house where you could play hide and seek for hours."

Onna took a breath, then continued.

"I remember playing with my brother Don, one time. We started the game right after breakfast. He said to me, 'go hide Onnie,' -- that's what he always called me, Onnie. People always said we were Donnie and Onnie. 'Go hide, Onnie, and I'll seek you!' Oh, I was sooo thrilled Donnie wanted to play with me. Usually, he just ignored me and called me a little pest. Well, my dear, I was in that hiding place until suppertime!"

Ravine rubbed her arms as the icy air settled around her. Then a low moaning noise began inside her head. She squinted her eyes, trying to ignore the dull pain. Onna didn't seem to notice anything, and kept smiling as she went on with her story.

"Well anyway, in the room where I slept, there was a big mirror like this one!"

"Go on," Ravine said. The pain was getting weaker.

"Well, the mirror my grandmother had was a bit smaller, and it was oval I think. Yes, most definitely oval, not squarish like this one."

"How much?" Ravine asked. It was getting late and Ravine needed to get home. But she didn't want to leave without the mirror.

"How much for what, dear?" Onna asked.

"The mirror. How much do you want for the mirror?"

She slowly stepped away from it and the air around her became warmer. She followed Onna to the till, and Ravine suddenly realized how warm the shop was.

"Well, considering how valuable it is, I'm sure it's got to be worth, oh, at least fifty dollars," Onna said. She stood behind the till tapping her long painted nails on the desk.

"Fifty dollars? But I don't have fifty dollars," Ravine said, panicking. She wanted the mirror. In fact, she was sure she needed this mirror, though she didn't know why.

"Yes, I know dear, antiques are expensive. But how about if I mark it down to twenty dollars? Just for you, my dear."

"All I have is eleven."

Ravine reached into her pocket, but all she found was a handful of change, two lint covered candies, and some crumpled up wrappers.

"You know, I think you are right. Eleven dollars is good," Onna said quickly, holding out her hand.

"Look, Onna, I forgot my allowance at home. I'll have to come back in tomorrow and get it."

Ravine looked back at the mirror.

"Can you save it for me?"

Onna shook her head. "I'm sorry, dear, but I can't do that. If I did that for you, then I'd have to do that for everyone. I'm sure you can understand the position that would put me in. I'd have things all around my store being saved. Heavens, how would I even keep track of it all?"

The grandfather clock started to chime five o'clock, and Ravine said she had to get home. But she'd be back, either tomorrow or Saturday.

By Friday, Derek was feeling better. There hadn't been any more mysterious phone calls, so far as he knew, and his mother seemed to be less agitated. There were a few times he thought she wanted to discuss something with him, but then Danielle would walk into the room, or the phone would ring. But at least they seemed to be normal calls. No whispering and turning her back toward him.

Ravine didn't get back to the store on Friday because her mother wanted her to come home from school straight away. But she awoke early Saturday morning, got dressed quickly, and headed down to the kitchen. Her parents were already there, in their pajamas, drinking coffee and reading the newspaper.

"Dad and I were thinking of going out for breakfast. Do you want to come?"

Ravine grabbed some bread. The white squishy stuff, not the healthy stuff that looked like it was full of birdseed. She opened the cupboards in search of the peanut butter. Not the pure, no sugar, no salt kind her parents liked; but real peanut butter, swirled with grape jelly.

"I'll pass. Derek and I are going to hang out today. I'm going to meet him at the school yard."

She sat down at the table and gobbed copious amounts of peanut butter and jelly on her bread. Then she dug her knife into the jar to get more. Her parents watched as she licked the knife with her tongue.

"That really is a disgusting habit, Ravine," her mother commented. "I wish you wouldn't do that. It's bad enough you insist on eating that awful stuff. You don't need to be cutting your tongue off, too."

"Sorry," Ravine tried to say, but it just came out as a grunt. She had already shoved in so much, and a big blob of peanut butter was sticking to the roof of her mouth.

"If you're not coming, we'll leave the door unlocked then," her father said, standing up. He was still in his housecoat, and headed upstairs to get dressed.

Ravine listened to the tinkle of the bell as she opened the door to *Maybe Antiques*. It looked like a busy morning. Onna waved to her, and Ravine's heart began to race. Onna was standing in front of the mirror with a young couple.

"Hi Onna," said Ravine, interrupting the conversation.

"Good morning, my dear. These nice people are the O'Neils, and they are interested in purchasing the old mirror. They have offered me fifteen dollars for it."

"Twenty," Ravine blurted out.

The O'Neils looked at her, surprised.

"I'll give you twenty for it, Onna. It really is a special mirror. Remember you told me that? You know how much I like it, and I've been coming here every day to look at it. Please, Onna, I told you I'd come back today and buy it."

Turning to the O'Neils, Onna agreed. "Oh, yes. It certainly is special. And this young girl comes in here a lot, and I know she really likes it. But you seem to like it, too. I remember having one just like this when I was younger. It's funny how I have forgotten so many things over the years but some things just – "

"Twenty-five dollars. We will give you twenty-five dollars for it," Mrs. O'Neil said, looking at Ravine.

Her husband gently grabbed her arm and whispered. "Don't you think that's a bit much, Melanie?"

"Thirty-five," Ravine blurted out.

"Let the kid have it, Melanie. It obviously means a lot to her if she is willing to pay that kind of cash for it. We'll head over to that other antique shop around the corner."

Ravine watched the young couple as they left the store. She dug into her jeans pocket, suddenly panicked that she hadn't brought enough money. She had three weeks of allowance, for sure; but she had also just grabbed some bills out of the jar she kept hidden behind the dictionary on her desk. She started counting. Thirty-six dollars. She was glad the bidding war hadn't gone on too long.

This was a lot of money, and she knew that was going to make the lecture from her mother even worse. But she was sure that it was worth it. Something she couldn't explain, some feeling, was telling her she needed to have this mirror.

"How are you going to get the mirror home, my dear?"

They both walked closer to the mirror and Ravine could feel the air get colder as she approached.

When Ravine lifted it, she wasn't surprised by the coldness of the frame. It wasn't quite as heavy as it looked, but it was awkward because it was taller than her.

"I'll carry it," Ravine said. The dull ache started again in her head.

Onna opened the front door for her, and watched as Ravine stumbled.

"Careful, dear. Enjoy your mirror!"

Ravine pushed her way through another group of customers that were just arriving at the store coming in the door, trying to be careful not to bump into anything or anybody. One elderly gentleman held the door open for her as stepped onto the porch. Passersby seemed amused by her carrying a mirror bigger than she was.

Ravine lived four blocks from the shop. After one block, her arms started to ache. After two blocks, she stumbled a few times and missed the curb. So she put it down, and rested for a few minutes. As she picked it up again, she caught a glimpse of a reflection in the glass out of the corner of her eye, and was so startled she almost dropped the mirror.

The reflection was not hers.

She looked again, and all she saw was herself.

But she knew the reflection a few seconds ago was not her.

Ravine's heart pounded loudly inside her chest as she hurried past the Morgan house, and awkwardly looked both ways before crossing the street. She passed Derek's house, but he wasn't in his yard.

She was sure he would want to see this mirror now.

As she shuffled up the driveway, Ravine realized the pain in her head was gone. But her arms were killing her.

She continued to grip the mirror tightly, and climbed the three steps to the front door. Before going in, she paused, trying to catch her breath.

Oh no! The car was in the garage. That meant her parents were already back from their breakfast out. She hoped they wouldn't hear her come in, and she could get the mirror upstairs without being seen.

Ravine turned the handle as quietly as she could, balancing the mirror on her foot, and pushed the door open with her elbow. She tried to steady the mirror, but it banged against the door jamb, chipping the paint.

"Oh great!" She hoped her father wouldn't see it.

"Is that you, Ravine?" her mother called from the kitchen.

Ravine stumbled through the door, and leaned the mirror against the wall in the entranceway.

"Yes, Mom, it's me."

Her mother came out to see her, drying her hands on a tea towel.

"What in heaven's name is that?" she gasped.

Ravine was sitting, cross-legged and smiling. "It's a mirror," Ravine said, simply.

Her mother stood with one hand on her hip.

"I can see it's a mirror, Ravine! What's it doing in our house?" She knew she didn't have to ask the next few questions. But she did anyway.

"Where did it come from? And what on earth do you plan to do with it? And why is it so ugly?"

Here we go, Ravine thought.

"I got it at *Maybe Antiques*," she said, meekly.

Her mother's frown deepened the lines between her eyes.

"Why, Ravine? Why? How many times have I told you not to waste your money in that run down place?"

"It's not junk! And it's my money. I should be able to spend my money however I want!" Ravine yelled back in frustration.

"Of course it's junk! Why do you think it's called 'Maybe' *Antiques*?"

Ravine just stared at her, so her mother continued.

"Because there aren't any antiques there anymore, that's why. Maybe there was when Ollie was still alive, but not now."

"I don't care, Mom. I like the mirror. It's…it's… special," Ravine replied.

"You know, if you keep spending your money on junk, your room will start looking like that shop," her mother replied.

They stared at each other, and then her mother gave a defeated sigh.

Ravine knew what that simple sigh meant. She knew her mother wished Ravine was more like other girls her age. Other eleven year-old girls were fussing with their hair, buying designer jeans, and spending their allowance on magazines and jewelry. But not Ravine. Oh no, Ravine could never be like that. She couldn't be a normal girl.

Ravine sat on the carpet, wiping the mirror with her sleeve. The reflection in the mirror was just her, a girl with thick brown hair, and dark brooding eyes behind the glasses. The girl looking back was slender, and shorter than most girls her age. But Ravine wasn't interest in her appearance. She liked her torn jeans and t-shirts, and she always hid her long hair under a baseball cap.

"I'm afraid to ask, but how much did you pay for it?"

"Thirty-five bucks. Onna wanted fifty, but I only paid thirty-five. Don't you think that's a bargain?"

Ravine looked up and smiled.

"Thirty-five dollars? Thirty-five dollars on junk? That's more than three weeks of your allowance gone!"

When Ravine didn't reply, her mother just shook her head.

"Take it upstairs, before your father sees it," she said. Then her mother disappeared back into the kitchen, still shaking her head.

Ravine stumbled backwards, dragging the mirror up each and every stair. The mirror thudded loudly and Ravine could picture the displeased look on her mother's face as the noise echoed throughout the house.

She closed her bedroom door and stood the mirror up against the wall beside her closet.

Ravine stared at the mirror for a long time.

"Who are you?" she finally stammered. Ravine backed away from the glass. She had seen someone else looking back at her on the way home from Onna's shop, so she knew there was somebody in there, even though the reflection had quickly disappeared.

Here in Ravine's bedroom, though, the stranger smiled silently.

It was a young girl with champagne hair, and bangs hanging over her sapphire eyes. This was the same image she had seen in her dream last Saturday.

"Who are you?" Ravine stammered again.

Chapter 3

The sun had finally reappeared from behind the purple grey clouds, and a last gust of wind left the leaves dancing briefly in the air, before descending slowly to the ground.

Derek sat in his room, staring out the window at the construction site across the street. In front of the house next to it, the Morgan kids played hopscotch.

It's funny, he thought. All my life that big empty lot scared me because of the spooky old house. Yet when he found out the house wasn't really there, that it wasn't visible to anybody except him and Ravine, his fears disappeared. Eventually, after he and Ravine had helped the ghost who lived in the house find peace, the house disappeared too.

Everybody had always said the empty lot at 56 Water Street was haunted. But for him and Ravine, the lot wasn't empty. And just a few months earlier, they had finally worked up the nerve and ventured into the invisible house, apparently summoned there by the ghost, Isabel. He felt sad that the house was gone now, but glad that they were able to help Isabel solve her mystery.

Still, that one adventure was enough for him. He didn't want to see things no one else saw. He didn't want to be helping ghosts, or hearing sounds that no else heard. He just wanted to be a normal kid. Well, a smart one, maybe. And good at sports. But basically just a normal kid.

As he stared out the window, he could see Ravine struggling to carry a big ugly mirror as she crossed the street. He groaned. This must be the thing she was talking about at school all week long, the piece of junk she wanted him to see at *Maybe Antiques*. And somehow he knew this thing was going to cause trouble and interfere with him being just a normal kid.

Derek closed the curtain, and flopped down on his bed.

He glanced at the photograph of him and Mike Markle taken when Derek won first prize in a drawing and essay contest in August. The famous illustrator had spent the day with him, giving him tips on drawing techniques and encouraging him to make the most of his talent.

Derek opened his night table drawer and took out the newspaper article about the contest. Ravine had been so excited for him that she bought a dozen copies of the paper to make sure all their friends saw it. She made Derek sign the article and she gave a copy to Mrs. Tackle, the teacher who had encouraged him to enter the contest.

He placed the article carefully back into the drawer, and reached over to pick up his basketball. He just held it for a while, and rolled it around in his hands. Still lying on his back, he started throwing the ball up at the ceiling.

His mind drifted. He thought about the summer that was now gone, and about the invisible house that was gone too. He thought about Ravine and her stupid mirror, and he thought that he really didn't want to get involved in another of her supernatural adventures. He thought about basketball, and he thought about the Halloween dance that was only a week away. He and Ravine were going together as Frankenstein and his Bride, and they were making their own costumes. His was almost done, but he didn't know if Ravine had even started hers. He sure hoped so.

But mostly he thought about his mother's recent strange behaviour, and all the secret phone calls.

By now, he was bouncing the basketball off the

ceiling. Lost somewhere in his thoughts, he didn't hear his mother from the bottom of the stairs yelling to him. And he didn't hear her footsteps in the hallway heading toward his closed door. He didn't even hear her open the door.

She flung it open and glared at him.

"Derek!"

He heard that, though. It startled him, but not nearly as much as when the basketball came down on his face and bounced off his nose. He cried out in pain.

"Now, that wouldn't have happened if you hadn't been throwing that thing at the ceiling."

He sat up rubbing his nose. It felt crooked. It's broken, he thought to himself.

"I'm sorry, mom. I forgot," he said. He tried to grin his best sheepish grin, but his nose hurt too much. The angry look on his mother's face didn't vanish.

"Yes, well … don't let it happen again." She walked over and handed him the telephone. "It's Ravine." Then she left, closing the door behind her.

"What's with the mirror?" Derek asked, without saying hello.

"How did you know?"

"I saw you from my bedroom window."

"Come over. I want you to take a look at it," Ravine said.

Derek really didn't want to know anything about the mirror. He had been in that store once before, with his mother, back when Oliver Owen was still alive. But he could never understand some of the junk Ravine bought there. He guessed that buying something bigger than herself probably cost Ravine a lot of money. And if she was willing to spend a lot of money on it, he thought, she must think it's pretty important. It looked heavy.

If it was worth spending all that money, he knew she was going to make a big deal out of it. He also knew that somehow this was going to involve him, and he really wasn't interested.

"Nah. I don't want to spend Saturday looking at myself in a junky old mirror. Let's go shoot some hoops instead."

"Ah c'mon, Derek. It's really special."

"No," he said harshly. Maybe a little too harshly, because Ravine was silent on the other end. He was about to say something when she replied, in a low quiet voice.

"Derek, I would really like you to come over. Just take a look at it. Then, if you still want to play basketball, we'll play basketball. Okay?"

Derek thought there was a tone of desperation in her voice, but he remained silent.

"Please, Derek."

"I'll be there in a few minutes," he replied. He knew she would just keep on bugging him if he didn't. But the sound of her voice told him this was a really big deal for her.

He hung up the phone and threw the basketball hard at the ceiling.

It didn't take long for Derek to appear, but he took his time crossing the street. He bounced the basketball between his legs as he strolled up Ravine's driveway.

Ravine closed her curtains as he got to her front door. She waited for her mother to get the door and send Derek upstairs. And she stared at the young girl in the mirror.

Closing her eyes, she waited for Derek. Just as she heard him climbing the stairs, she thought she heard the whisper of Isabel's voice.

"Never forget, Ravine."

Her eyes shot open, but she caught only a glimpse of a fading image in the mirror. She was sure that this time it had been Isabel's image.

Derek knocked at the bedroom door, and let himself in without waiting for an invitation.

"Okay, Ravine, show me this mirror you can't stop talking about." He forced out a laugh.

The mirror sat in the room lit by the afternoon sun. It looked like an ordinary mirror. The girl in the mirror had vanished.

"It's nothing," she said. "Let's go shoot some hoops."

She grabbed Derek's basketball and he followed her out of the room, puzzled, but shutting the door behind him.

"What happened to your nose? It looks like you walked into something."

He told her what happened, feeling a little foolish about it and trying not to let on how much his nose hurt.

"So what's so special about this mirror?" he asked, as he tossed the basketball to Ravine.

Anybody who ever said 'you throw like a girl' had never met Ravine. Derek was a good basketball player, but he had to admit that Ravine was better. She was smaller than most kids her age, but she could beat almost anybody at just about any game. He wished he had her knack.

Ravine passed the ball back to Derek. "You just have to see it, that's all. There is something very interesting about it. But it's gone now, and I don't know when it'll be back."

Derek shot the ball at the basket and watched as it teetered before going in. He picked up the ball and walked over to Ravine, spinning the ball on the tip of his finger.

"You're making no sense," he said to her, watching the ball spin.

She grabbed the ball from him and they stood in the schoolyard staring at each other. Derek seemed to be in the middle of a growth spurt, and he was a whole head taller than her now.

"I am making sense. And I'd make a lot more sense if you'd pay attention to what I've been trying to tell you," she said raising her voice. "What's your problem anyway? You've been real miserable lately."

Suddenly, the wind picked up from nowhere, whipping dirt and leaves around their faces and feet. Derek and Ravine stood with their arms shielding their eyes. Ravine lowered her eyes to the ground, waiting for the wind to stop. Derek had new pink shoelaces.

They stood staring at each other. Ravine was suddenly unsure what to say. They had both seen 56 Water Street, and they had both seen Isabel. But what if Derek couldn't see anything in the mirror except himself?

"There's a girl in the mirror," she said quietly.

"And I bet she's a brown-haired short-stuff with glasses," he laughed.

Ravine, repeated what she had just said. This time slower, and quieter.

"There's a girl in the mirror. With blonde hair. I don't have blonde hair."

Derek dropped the basketball and it rolled onto the grass. He quickly went after it and bounced it back toward Ravine.

"What?"

"Oh, for crying out loud! I know it sounds crazy, but I'm telling you the truth. There is a girl in the mirror. Onna doesn't see her, but I do and I bet you will too. But she's gone right now, and I don't know when she'll be back."

Derek took a step away from Ravine. This was exactly what he didn't want to get involved in. This was not normal kid stuff.

"I'm not crazy, Derek. I saw her reflection when I was carrying the mirror home. Then she was there after I got it up to my room. Smiling at me. I am not crazy," she said, desperately trying to convince herself of that. "She was there."

Derek looked Ravine in the eyes. He knew she

wasn't crazy. They had experienced something out of this world during the summer, so he had no doubt what she was saying was true. But he definitely did not want to get involved with ghosts and spirits again. Once was enough for him.

He had told her, even while the mystery of Isabel Roberts and 56 Water Street was unraveling, that he just wanted to be a normal kid. When their friend Madeline told them they were special, he didn't want to hear that either. He hoped that once Isabel was gone, there would be no more spooky mysteries. The last thing he wanted was to look into this mirror and see somebody else.

They walked back to Ravine's house and Derek listened to Ravine tell him what happened at *Maybe Antiques*. Anybody listening would have thought they were playing a game of make-believe.

Ravine opened her bedroom door, and together they entered and approached the mirror.

To Derek, the old mirror just looked like junk. But if Ravine said she could see a reflection of a girl, he knew she was telling the truth.

"Where is she?" Derek asked, seeing only the reflections of Ravine and himself.

"I don't know," Ravine said, looking at their

reflections. "She was here earlier, but she disappeared just before you got here."

Ravine moved closer to the mirror. She had been standing slightly behind Derek, a little off to one side. She pressed her fingers against the glass. The mirror was cold and smooth. It reminded her of ice, but not wet. She pulled her hand away.

Derek put his hand up to the glass. "It's so cold," he said, running his hand down the glass and then in a slow circular motion. The glass became brighter and colder the more Derek rubbed his hand over it. It felt like a bright cold winter's day.

"You do believe me, don't you?" Ravine asked. She was beginning to doubt herself, and wondered if her imagination had created this whole thing.

Derek sat on the bed next to Ravine, staring at the mirror and waiting for something to happen.

"Yeah, I believe you," Derek said at last. But still the girl did not reappear.

Derek became restless and started to fidget. He didn't like the fact that there could be things around them that Ravine could see and he could not. But he also didn't like that they both could see things no one else could. He just wanted to be normal.

"Maybe this mystery is just for you," he said hopefully.

"Oh, Derek. I have to know what this is all about, and I need you to help me."

"No."

"What?"

"I said no. I'm glad we helped Isabel, but the only ghosts and goblins I ever want to see again is at the Halloween dance."

"Derek, please!"

"No."

Ravine was angry, but she tried not to show it. She was hoping that she would be able to convince him to help.

"Look, I have to be going," Derek said.

Ravine nodded.

"Those are silly looking shoelaces," she said.

"No they're not. They're cool!"

"They're girly laces," she said.

"But you like pink. It's your favourite colour. You wear it all the time."

"Yeah, but it's a girl colour."

"As if you ever act like a girl!"

Ravine thought about hauling off and slugging him, but decided if she wanted his help that wouldn't be a good idea. So she said nothing.

She was disappointed when Derek got up to leave. It was almost supper, he said, but Ravine knew that he was getting restless staring at himself.

She watched him from her window, bouncing the basketball home. When Ravine couldn't see him anymore, she turned away from the window.

There she was.

Just like before, at the top right hand corner of the mirror. Smiling.

Ravine didn't want to move too quickly, afraid the girl might disappear again. She whispered Derek's name even though he was not there.

Then, unlike before, the image of the girl moved to the middle of the mirror and Ravine could now see her entire body.

Her slender frame was hidden beneath a long blue dress. The dress looked old-fashioned and ordinary, maybe even a bit tattered. She wore a white bib apron tied in a large bow behind her back. She looked like an illustration Ravine had seen of *Alice in Wonderland*. From her clothes, it was easy to tell that she came from a poor family. But despite that, she wore what looked like an expensive gold locket in the shape of a heart, dangling from a silver thread around her neck.

"What's your name?" Ravine whispered. But instead of answering, the girl just moved further back into the mirror. She waved Ravine to follow as she slowly faded in and out of view.

Not wanting to let the girl go, Ravine instinctively

reached out to touch the mirror. To her surprise, her hand went through the cold glass. Not like the glass had broken, but like when you put your hand in water. Ravine could feel herself being pulled in to the mirror by some invisible force.

The girl suddenly disappeared, and Ravine's hand was back in the real world once more. The mirror was cold hard glass again.

Ravine backed away from the mirror, shaking uncontrollably. Cold, but dry, her skin tingled in the warmth of her room. She sat on the bed gaping at the redness of her hand and fingers. Her heart pounded loudly against her chest, and she took a couple of deep breaths, trying to calm herself.

She was excited, but didn't feel at all frightened. She didn't even feel there was anything impossible about what had just happened.

She gazed at the mirror, but it was only herself looking back.

Who was the girl in the mirror?

Derek sat on the couch. At the other end, his teenage sister, Danielle, was yapping on the phone. He was trying to watch television, and he was not very happy. She could take the telephone anywhere, but the television was pretty much fixed in one spot.

So he turned up the volume.

Danielle spoke louder.

Up went the volume again.

Danielle got even louder.

Derek added more volume until Danielle practically had to yell into the phone.

The war of sound ended quickly when their mother came barging into the living room. Without a word, she switched off the television and hung up the phone.

"Why'd you do that? I was talking to Jeffrey!"

"Well, now you're not," their mother said.

Danielle turned and glared at Derek, her eyes on fire.

It was time to leave, he thought, and he quickly headed upstairs, retreating to his bedroom. He closed the door behind him.

He looked out the window, but nothing much seemed to be happening in the street. He had an idea, and picked up his sketchpad. Maybe he would draw a series of sketches of the construction across the road. He had already won a contest with his drawing of the old house that used to be there, the one that was invisible to everyone except him and Ravine. Keeping a record of what replaces it might be fun, he thought.

But the construction crew wasn't working today,

and the Morgan kids were gone. So he quickly lost interest in the sketch and picked up his basketball instead. Flopping down on the bed, he started to throw it toward the ceiling. Then he remembered the earlier lecture, and his sore nose, and stopped.

He wondered if Ravine was still sitting in her room and still staring at her reflection. He realized he had forgotten to ask if she had done any work on her Halloween costume. But his mind drifted back to this morning when he had walked in on his mother and another of those mysterious phone calls. She seemed annoyed and frustrated with the person on the other end. He thought it sounded like she was being forced into agreeing to something she didn't really want to do.

But, once again, she had ended the call when Derek appeared, and dismissed his questions about who she was talking to.

Ravine ate supper in silence, staring at the empty seat across from her. Rachel's seat. It was never discussed, but out of habit no one sat there any more.

Her thoughts drifted to Derek's crankiness, then to her mirror and the unknown girl who smiled at her from inside the mirror, then back to Derek, then to the mirror again. Back and forth. One time the girl was looking back at her, the next she saw only her own reflection.

Then she thought about Derek's behaviour over the past little while. She wasn't sure how long it had been going on, but he didn't seem to be himself lately. Oh, she wasn't surprised that he didn't want anything to do with the mirror. And she was sure she could convince him to change his mind, that wasn't a problem. But he seemed somehow to be more quiet and withdrawn, even though he was continuing to act more or less like he always did. She could sense there was some kind of sadness or trouble going on in his head.

"What do you think about that?"

Ravine looked up.

"I don't think she heard you, Robbie," said her mother.

Ravine shook her head.

"We were talking about next summer. We're thinking about renting a motor home and driving to the east coast," said her dad.

"Sure. That sounds like fun."

Her parents continued to talk, and Ravine drifted in and out of the conversation. She realized it would be the first family vacation since Rachel's death.

Then, just like the night before, a sudden scream

briefly filled her head. It was intense at first, but quickly softened into a quiet ringing in her ears that she could only barely make out. But it was there, and she was sure it was connected with the girl in the mirror. It had to be.

After the table was cleared and the dishes done, Ravine slipped away. She closed her bedroom door and sat on the floor with her homework.

She tried to do the math, but soon realized she was just doodling in the margins of the paper. She was drawing little pictures of a mysterious girl with champagne hair. Not that anyone else would have recognized what she was drawing. She was no artist. For that, you needed Derek.

She soon grew tired of pretending that she was doing her homework. Looking behind her, the mirror stood against the wall, almost as if it was waiting for something. Or someone.

Ravine stood up and walked to the mirror. With the soft touch of her fingers, the mirror began to glow. At first it was a soft and faint light, but then it grew into a brilliant translucent blue.

The girl appeared, coming quickly into focus. She was smiling, and beckoning Ravine to follow her.

Cautiously, Ravine inched her arm toward the

mirror. Like before, her hand slipped into the cold glass like she was putting it into water. She could feel a tug on her arm that seemed to want to pull her whole body into the mirror. She resisted a little, but soon just let the invisible force pull her. Gently, she felt herself being pulled into the mirror. She seemed to have no control over this, and she had no feeling that she should be fighting back. For some reason, none of this seemed to be at all strange or scary.

With a sudden flash that would only have been seen by someone standing in her room, Ravine disappeared into the mirror.

She had no idea where she was, and she couldn't see the young girl.

What now, she thought.

She didn't feel at all frightened.

She tried calling out to the girl, but she didn't know what name to call. So she just kept repeating 'hello, where are you'. There was no reply, and there was nothing around her. She seemed to be standing in space, not on anything, or in anything. Just standing. There was whiteness all around her. Even though she didn't seem to be moving, there was still a feeling that she was being tugged somewhere.

Then the whiteness began to deepen into shades

of grey, before slowly turning into total blackness. She never imagined anything could ever be so black, and that made her uncomfortable. Ever since she was very small, she had always been a little afraid of the dark. After Rachel died, the dark always seemed a little darker to Ravine, and a little more frightening.

Suddenly, the pulling sensation stopped and let her go. With a thud, she fell on something hard and cold. It didn't hurt at all, but she had definitely hit something pretty solid.

Slowly she opened her eyes. Despite the warm air, she was shivering.

It took a couple of minutes to shake the pins and needles out of her arms and legs, and she looked around to see where she was.

That didn't help much.

She was sitting on a scuffed up wooden floor, but it didn't look like any place she had ever seen. It was still too dark to make out anything clearly, so she thought the best thing to do was sit and wait. Not that there was much else she could do anyway.

After a while, she thought the darkness was starting to lift, and she hoped she'd soon be able to see better.

Then, almost immediately, she fell asleep. But

just before she did, she wondered again where she was.

Ravine's head felt stuffy. She had no idea how long she had been asleep, but she must have been sweating because she felt damp all over. Then she remembered: She had gone through the mirror, and she had no idea where she was right now.

She was still feeling more curious than worried, so she got up slowly and brushed herself off. She crossed her arms over her chest, rubbing them briskly because she was chilly.

As she finally took a small step forward, the wooden floor creaked loudly under her feet.

"Is that you, Abigail?" A slight woman with an apron tied around her waist walked into the kitchen. Ravine could clearly see now that she was in a kitchen. The woman was drying her hands on a towel, thoughtfully looking around the room. Ravine had no idea who this woman was, and it took a moment to realize that the woman didn't seem at all surprised to see Ravine.

She studied the older woman. Her long grey cotton dress looked clean, but old, and the stained white apron had certainly seen better days. She was tall, or at least she seemed tall to Ravine, with a pretty and kindly face. Her hair was champagne coloured.

The woman continued to ignore Ravine.

They were in one large room, and there was a long wooden table that divided it into kitchen and living room. The woman walked back to the kitchen side and sat at the table. Ravine followed slowly, taking the seat opposite.

Neither of them said anything, so Ravine studied the woman's face. She thought again that it looked kindly, but there was an obvious sign of sadness in her eyes. The woman tucked her long hair behind her ears, but it didn't stay there, so she tucked it again.

Ravine suddenly realized the woman couldn't see her, and felt sorry for her. Blindness must be a terrible thing, she thought.

"Can you hear me?" Ravine whispered, afraid of her own voice.

No reaction. The woman just sat, facing toward the screen door and tucking her hair behind her ears again.

Ravine spoke a second time, but a little louder. Still no reaction.

Once more she tried, before finally deciding the woman was both blind and deaf.

With her legs shaking, Ravine stood and slowly

walked around the table, leaning one hand on it for support. The woman continued to sit facing the door.

Ravine gazed out the kitchen window. Nothing looked familiar. The rolling hills went out to the horizon, and at one side of the pasture a few trees loomed over a barn. A thick forest stretched out behind the barn, wrapping around one side of the house. Ravine didn't think she had ever seen such tall trees.

Absolutely none of this was familiar.

Now fear gripped her.

She closed her eyes and began to panic. She tried to steady herself against the wall, and after a few minutes she calmed down.

But she still didn't know where she was, or how she was going to get home.

Ravine moved away and turned to look at the room again. A sideboard holding plates and cups stood next to the window. The big wooden table was in the centre of the room, about midway between the window and the fireplace. Even though there was also a large wood-burning stove in the kitchen, it was obvious that the fireplace was used for cooking too. There were lots of pots and pans, heavy things that looked like they were made from iron, hanging from the mantel above the stone hearth.

Smoke stains around the hearth and on the ceiling of the room showed that both the stove and the fireplace were probably used for warmth. Ravine could only guess at that, though, because she didn't know if wherever she was ever got cold enough to need fires for warmth. All she could tell for sure was that today the sun was shining, the windows were open, and pale yellow curtains danced lightly, letting in a gentle breeze.

Ravine didn't know what to do. If she were to suddenly touch this deaf and blind woman to get her attention, how would the woman react? She assumed there must be at least one other person who lived here, because the woman had called out for Abigail. But no one else was here now, and the woman would certainly know that.

Looking around, Ravine noticed how sparsely the cabin was furnished. Besides the wooden table, there were four chairs. The chairs had fancy padding on the seats, but the fabric was worn and faded. A dark red wooden rocker sat near the front window, but its paint was chipped and peeling. It was the same colour as the wall of death in Onna's shop.

A large wooden spinning wheel sat the other side of the front window. Next to that was a white cradle that looked as if it had recently been painted. A rifle hung on a rack by the front door.

Ravine noticed the door to the front porch looked like a screen door, except there was no screen in it. There were no pictures or other decorations on the walls, no flowers. Of course, why would a blind woman have flowers and pictures, she thought. But what about the other people who must live here?

Ravine stepped carefully around the room. She cringed as the floorboards creaked under her feet, but the woman took no notice. She sat peacefully, with her hands in her lap, facing the back door.

Ravine brushed her hand against the hardness of the rocker, and then felt the softness of the white blanket folded inside the cradle. Where was the baby, she wondered?

Above the living area, Ravine saw a tiny loft. Without hesitating, she climbed the ladder.

The loft was even smaller than it looked from floor level. It's ceiling was slanted, following what Ravine assumed was the line of the building's roof. There was a single bed in the loft, neatly made with a cream-coloured cotton cover. Ravine sat on the edge of the bed and could feel the floor underneath her as she sank into the mattress. Outside the small window, a huge oak tree loomed over the house. A few branches poked between the curtains and into the open window. A sudden stiff breeze sent the light fabric into a tizzy before it was caught on a branch.

Ravine could tell this was not a house with a lot of money. She also knew that this was not a house like anything she had ever seen. This is what she imagined homes looked like long ago, way back before she was born. Probably even before her parents or grandparents were born.

If she was right, how did she get here? And how could she get out of here? She had never seen anything like this, and Ravine wondered if she had traveled back in time. She tried to keep her thoughts clear and focused.

She stood up, grateful that she was short enough not to bang her head on the low ceiling, and turned toward the other end of the room.

In the corner, large and foreboding, was a mirror. Her mirror.

Ravine was stunned. She stood, unable to move, staring in disbelief. This wasn't a similar mirror; it was the same one. She was sure of it.

When she could finally move, she approached the mirror. It glowed just as it had in Onna's shop. Her heart pounded against her chest.

Just then, she heard footsteps coming up the porch steps and she looked down into the main room. It didn't register with her that the deaf woman had also heard the footsteps. She watched as a champagne-haired girl swung open the door.

"I'm home, Mama," the girl's voice rang out.

"Abigail Baldwin, where have you been? You should have been home forty-five minutes ago!"

Ravine gasped, it was the girl from the mirror. Ravine stumbled backwards and fell against the cold glass and disappeared.

Chapter 4

Dawn.

Outside, the darkness began to fade and the sky gradually turned to day, leaving a heavy blanket of fog. A light dusting of frost covered the grass.

Inside, Ravine rolled over and felt soft flannel sheets beneath her. A feather pillow cradled her head as her face sunk deeper into softness. She opened her eyes slowly, wondering where she was.

She sat up quickly, startled to find herself safe and warm in her own room, in her own bed. Putting her hands to her head, Ravine tried to remember how she had gotten back.

Or had she been anywhere except right here in her own bed?

No. It couldn't have been just a dream. She remembered putting her hand through the mirror. She remembered the feeling of the tug on her arm. And she remembered the cabin.

She closed her eyes again, desperately trying to recall every detail after she had been swallowed up by the mirror.

It must have been a dream, she thought, shaking her head. What else could it have been?

Ravine turned her gaze toward the mirror, and a chill swept over her.

No. It was real. She did go through the mirror. She was in that house. She did see that woman and the young girl. And she did fall back through the mirror.

Abigail Baldwin.

The name echoed inside Ravine's head. That was the name she and Derek had noticed in the cemetery during the summer. She remembered seeing the grave when they were searching for Isabel. Something about that grave had made them stop, and they had wondered what happened to this ten-year-old girl. Then a few days ago she got a shock from that gravestone. And her new mirror was from some Baldwin family.

Now the girl was smiling at her, from inside the mirror in the middle of Ravine's room. And now that she knew the girl's name, she was sure this must be the same girl who is buried in Summerhill Cemetery.

She flung off the covers, hopped out of bed, and

walked across her room. The floor was cold beneath her feet. She touched her hand against the glass and quickly pulled away. It was cold too.

Derek was in his room putting the finishing touches on his Frankenstein costume. He tried to pay attention to what he was doing, but his mind wasn't really on it. He was distracted by another one of his mother's secret phone calls. When he got up this morning, he heard her soft voice whispering as he passed her bedroom. He stood outside the open door to listen.

"A year? First it was just for the summer. And now you're saying a year?"

His mother's voice was hoarse. There was a short silence before she continued.

"No. We haven't received it yet. But when it comes, I'll give it to him."

Silence again.

"No, I am not trying to keep him from you."

Silence.

"No. I am not going to persuade him one way or another. He can make up his own mind."

As she hung up the receiver, she turned and saw Derek watching her. She offered no explanation, and he didn't ask. There had been a lot of these mysterious calls, and she always brushed him off when he asked about them. He didn't see any point in asking again. He knew there was something going on. He just hoped that whatever it was it would soon be over, and that it didn't mean trouble for anyone.

He tried to focus on his costume. There sure wasn't anything original about it, he thought. He was going as Frankenstein, with Ravine going as his Bride. But he was hoping they could both do a good enough job on these costumes to win a prize. Unfortunately, his injured nose wasn't going to help them. He touched it and winced with the pain. But even though he had been sure it broke when the basketball hit him in the face, it didn't look crooked. It wasn't even bruised.

But it sure did hurt still.

Ravine promised him her costume would be finished in plenty of time. But he had a sinking feeling that it wouldn't be. She was consumed by that silly mirror. She was probably in her room right now staring at it, waiting for some mystery girl to show up. When Ravine got focused on something, she lost sight of everything else. It would be just like her to forget all about the Halloween party.

Derek worked away at his costume, with his

mind drifting. His thoughts roamed all over, when a loud knock at his door jolted him back to reality.

"What are you doing?" Ravine asked, coming in without being invited.

Derek held up his costume.

"Awesome!" Ravine said. "That's great! Where did you get this stuff from," she asked, feeling the pants Derek stitched together. "Cool material." The pants were black, and made out of a material that looked like metal. And he had found a metallic looking long-sleeved turtleneck in dark grey.

"At the second hand store up town. How's your costume?"

"Not done yet. But it will be."

"Ravine, you do remember that there's a history quiz on Friday? And a math test on Tuesday? When are you going to have time to do the costume?"

"Don't stress," she said. "It'll get done."

Ravine watched Derek as he put everything away.

"Do you want to come to the cemetery with me?"

Derek stopped what he was doing and stared at her. His eyebrows creased together and he frowned.

"This has to do with that mirror of yours, doesn't it?"

Ravine nodded.

"No," Derek said, throwing his costume in the closet and slamming the door.

"No, what?" Ravine asked.

"No, I don't want to go to the cemetery," he said loudly.

"Why not? What's your problem lately? You're acting so weird."

"Nothing, I just don't want to go to the cemetery. Do you have a problem with that? If this was about visiting Rachel, that would be different. But it isn't, is it?"

Ravine opened the bedroom door to leave. She stopped to look at Derek.

"Actually, I do have a problem with that. We aren't normal," she said, "neither of us. And there's nothing you can do about it. This summer should have convinced you about that."

She slammed the door behind her.

Derek watched Ravine from his window. She walked quickly, and he could tell she was crying. He watched as she wiped her cheek on a sleeve and burst into a run.

He sat on the bed, angry with himself. He and Ravine had been inseparable forever, and all these years they never had any big fights. Not once.

He felt awful. Absolutely awful.

She was right. They weren't normal. And he was angry about that too. Normal was all he really wanted. He didn't ask to be anything special, and he wished it would just go away.

Ravine ran up her driveway, wiping the tears from her cheeks.

Her parents were sitting quietly in the living room, sharing the newspaper. Ravine hurried upstairs before they could see her tear-stained face.

She plopped down on her bed, still angry with Derek. He was acting strange lately, and he seemed so uptight and tense. She had heard him snapping at other people. And now this.

Her eyes were red and swollen and she let the tears flow freely.

When she wiped the last tear from her cheek, she grabbed a warm jacket. Well, if Derek doesn't want to go, then Derek doesn't have to. She was less angry now, but she was going to go without him.

She paused at her door before opening it, and looked at the mirror. It looked out of place in her small room, but she looked into it to see who was looking back. It was just her own reflection.

She knew that the visit to the strange house where Abigail Baldwin lived was real.

Ravine headed out of her room, closing the door softly behind her.

The ride to Summerhill Cemetery seemed longer than usual. The cold wind was whipping against her face, making her eyes create more tears. She was still mad at Derek, and making this trip alone only made it seem longer. By the time she finally made it up the last winding hill, her legs ached, her arms were sore, and she was out of breath.

She got off her bike, letting it fall, and flopped down beside a big old oak tree, still trying to catch her breath. Fallen leaves danced around her legs before settling into colourful piles beneath the tall trees.

Past the iron gates, the tombstones stood strong and silent.

The wind howled, whipping the dark grey clouds through the sky and blowing her hair around her face and into her eyes. She wished Derek was with her, and that only made her angry again.

She stood and headed up the path into the cemetery.

Ravine walked slowly, taking the same route she had with her parents a few nights ago. A soft mist filled the air, so light that at first she didn't notice it.

She started to pay attention when it quickly turned into a hard rain.

The rain pounded. In the distance, there were still areas of the sky that were blue and sunny, but clouds were swirling violently overhead and, at least where she was, the rain was heavy. Although it was hard to see now, she knew where she was going. She continued further into the cemetery, then stopped.

She ran her hand over the rough stone, feeling the same shock as she did a few days earlier. Silently, she mouthed the name and dates.

Abigail Baldwin, 1872-1882.

The gravestone was small. Humble.

No flowers.

No bushes.

But there were plenty of weeds.

The rain pelted down harder, making the last leaves of autumn cling to the trees, hanging limp and heavy from the branches.

Ravine covered her eyes with her arm as the wind started to swirl and grow stronger. The weather was starting to frighten her. She got down on her knees and wrapped her arms around Abigail's small tombstone as the wind whipped dirt and fallen leaves into the air. The storm didn't last long, but it was very intense.

A sudden crack of thunder startled Ravine and a bolt of lightning pierced the sky, followed by another crack of thunder.

Drenched and cold, Ravine leaned her face against the tombstone. Then, with a thunderous crash, everything went black.

Derek stood at the living room window watching the mid-afternoon storm. It was quite a show. Lightning filled the sky, and rain slashed down like tiny silver razor blades.

He shut the curtains. It was time to call Ravine.

When her mother answered the telephone, Derek knew instinctively that Ravine was out in this terrible storm. He knew where she had gone, and he wished he had gone with her.

"Oh, uh, hi, Mrs. Crawl. Is Ravine home?"

"I thought Ravine was with you," her mother said, sounding startled.

"No. Oh wait, I think she said she was going to Joannie's house this afternoon," he lied. "Thanks. I'll call her there." Then he hung up quickly.

He was angry at Ravine for being out in this weather, like somehow she had planned the storm all by herself. And he was angry with himself for not going with her.

He grabbed his coat and opened the front door.

"Where do you think you're going?"

Derek turned to face his mother.

"Just out," he said.

But she shook her head and closed the door.

"Not in this weather you're not, Mister."

"No, I guess not," he mumbled.

Ravine was lying, looking like a limp dishrag, in a puddle beside Abigail's grave. She rolled over, moaning. She tried to open her eyes, but her eyelids were coated with something sticky. She moaned again. But then she could hear voices. She tried to speak, but nothing came out.

"Aw, come on Meredith, please stop crying. You know how she gets distracted up in those woods. There's nothing up there to hurt her, She'll be along any minute now, you'll see."

"She's never been this late before, Abe, and it's dark."

"You know how she is, she'd forget her head if it weren't attached."

Ravine opened her eyes. The rain had stopped abruptly, but she was soaked and covered in mud. Struggling to sit up, she felt an aching in her arms and legs. She closed her eyes again briefly to see if the pounding in her head would ease. No luck. When she opened them again, she pressed her hand against her forehead and felt something warm and sticky.

Ravine started to sway when she saw her hand covered in blood. In a panic, she tried to stand, but quickly plunked herself back on the ground. Carefully, she put her head between her knees, hoping this would make the dizziness subside. It looked like a lot of blood to her, but she couldn't tell if it was a big cut. Worse, she had no idea when or how she had cut herself. But from the pounding in her head, she knew she had banged it on something.

Knowing she had a long ride ahead of her, she tried to get her head settled. Pressing her hand hard against her forehead seemed to make the bleeding stop, but she waited a few minutes to be sure it didn't start again. Minutes seemed like hours, but she managed finally to get up.

Still feeling unsteady on her feet, she thought she had better walk around for a bit before trying to get back onto her bike. She walked slowly and wobbly, moving down the path toward the gate where she had left her bike. When she decided she was feeling well enough to ride, she mounted her bike and coasted down the winding road that led away from the cemetery.

It was a slow ride home, but by the time she reached her driveway, the sun had come out between the few remaining clouds and a brilliant rainbow arced across a bright blue sky.

Ravine left her bike in the middle of the driveway and went up the stairs. The blood on her forehead was dried now, and she could feel a lump was forming on the side of her cheek.

Her mother opened the door.

"Where were you? Oh, in the name of heaven, what happened to you?"

She pulled Ravine into the kitchen and sat her down. Ravine felt a cold damp rag suddenly pressed up against her forehead.

"Ow! That hurts!"

Ravine tried to push her mother's hand away.

"Trust me. This will help," she said. She rinsed out the cloth and reapplied it. "So, what happened? You have a long cut above your left eye and a big bruise on your cheek."

Ravine was silent.

"Well?"

"I decided to go for a bike ride after I went to Derek's and I got caught in the storm. I couldn't see in the rain, and my tires slid in a puddle. I crashed, into a wall, I think."

Ravine kept her eyes down, looking at her lap as she told the story. Not entirely true. But not a lie either. She had gone for a bike ride, and for all she knew she did crash into a wall. Just not on her bike. She couldn't remember. But she couldn't tell her mother why she had gone for a ride in the first place.

"You're going to get into a hot bath, then have something to eat. Then you're going to get into nice warm pajamas, and stay inside."

Derek bounced his basketball off the ceiling. He was lying on his bed, not remembering that his mother would soon be up if he didn't stop.

I should probably call Ravine again to see if she's okay, he thought. No. If she isn't home, that will only make her mother worry.

He bounced the basketball off the ceiling.

I should probably call her to say I'm sorry, he thought. No. What should I feel sorry about? Because I didn't want to ride my bike to a cemetery? Because I didn't have any interest in her stupid mirror?

The ball hit the ceiling again.

No. There is nothing for me to apologize about.

I hope Ravine is okay, he thought.

The basketball thudded against the ceiling again, just as he heard his mother coming up the stairs.

After her bath and something to eat, she said she was feeling a lot better, though her head was still pounding. It hurt where she banged it, but she also had a real bad headache that wasn't from her injury.

Telling her mother she had some studying to do, she went upstairs to her room. She shut the door, and took out her math and history homework.

Sitting on the floor in front of the mirror, she gazed at her reflection. Her left cheek was swollen, and there was already a big purple bruise. She thought it was probably going to get bigger, and since she also had a cut on her forehead, she was pretty sure this was going to turn into a black eye.

Now that's a pretty sight, she thought. At least it'll look good for the Halloween party. I'll be able to look awful without make-up.

She stared at the bandage on her forehead. She still had no idea how she had injured herself.

She tried to focus on her books. There was a

history test the next day, but all the names and dates seemed to run together in her head, and her mind kept drifting off.

Abigail. Abe. Meredith. Abigail. Abe. Meredith.

The harder she tried to concentrate on her schoolwork, the louder the names echoed.

Abigail. Abe. Meredith.

Those were the names that belonged to the people she saw when she went through the mirror and found herself in some strange house or cabin.

She looked in the mirror, gazing at her reflection.

Abe. Meredith.

Abigail.

The girl was looking back from the mirror.

"What do you want from me?" Ravine asked. "What happened to you?"

Chapter 5

Derek sat at the kitchen table with his head propped up on his hands. His mood hadn't improved from yesterday, and he hadn't slept very well. From the corner of his eye, he watched his mother pack his lunch. She was chattering away about how busy the week was going to be for them. Derek just nodded in reply. And she reminded him it would still be two more days before he got his basketball back.

Danielle munched on a piece of toast, staring down at the table with the usual scowl on her face.

Everyday, without fail, he and Ravine walked to school together. It had been that way ever since they started kindergarten.

This morning, he slowly made his way down the front steps. There she was, on the other side of the street deliberately looking away and already just about at the corner. She hadn't waited for him.

Walking to school by himself, he kept his eyes on the ground as he started to walk quicker. When he came to a pile of leaves, he kicked his way through them and crunched them loudly under his feet. With his longer legs, he soon caught up and was even with her on the other side of the road.

He looked across the street, but Ravine did not look back.

He tried scuffing his feet on the sidewalk and coughing, but still Ravine did not look his way.

Ravine suddenly started into a slow trot and put more distance between them, disappearing down the laneway that led into the schoolyard.

When he got to the playground, Derek saw that Ravine was already in a group with Sunil, Joannie, and Lisa. All the kids were animated, and pointing at Ravine's face.

Ravine looked at him, but turned away quickly.

Derek gasped when he saw the swollen cheek and bandaged forehead. Joannie was touching it, and asking Ravine if it hurt.

Derek approached the group.

"Hey, guys, what's up?"

"Hey, Derek," Sunil said. "Do ya like my shoes?"

Derek looked at the fluorescent pink laces on Sunil's sneakers and laughed.

"Guess what?" Joannie said in obvious excitement. "We're having a DJ for the Halloween party," she added, without waiting for a guess.

"How do you know that?" Lisa asked.

"I heard Mrs. Tackle talking about it to Mr. Scott. And Mr. Scott is bringing in a disco ball!"

"Oh no, not a disco ball," Lisa groaned.

"Why, what's wrong with that?"

"My parents used to dance to those things. That is so lame. And old."

"What's a disco ball?" asked Sunil.

"Oh, it's this big shiny globe hanging from the ceiling with little mirrors all over it," said Joannie. "You shine a light on it while it spins and it makes beams of light fly all over the place. It's really old fashioned."

As they talked about Saturday's dance, Derek stole a quick glance at Ravine but she continued to ignore him. In fact, she seemed to be ignoring everyone, and Derek wondered what she was thinking. She looked distracted.

"Are you guys finished your costumes?" Derek asked.

Ravine looked the other way.

"Hey, Dude," said Sunil. "Wait till you see my costume. It's going to blow away the competition! First prize for costume is already in my pocket."

"I'm not quite done mine yet," Joannie said.

"Me neither, but there's still plenty of time left," Ravine added. She looked at Derek and gave him a dirty look. There was no mistaking that look, and everybody noticed it.

"So what happened to …?"

Just as Derek was about to ask how Ravine hurt her face, the bell rang. Ravine didn't hesitate, and immediately headed off to the line. As usual, everyone else dawdled.

The rest of the kids looked at Derek. There was obviously something wrong between Derek and Ravine, but that was so completely outside anyone's experience that none of them seemed to know what to say. Joannie and Lisa headed to the line together, and Derek and Sunil fell in behind them, no one saying a word.

Just as they got to the door, Sunil piped up. "I don't know, dude. A disco ball sounds pretty cool to me."

As soon as everyone was seated, Mrs. MacDonald rolled up the world map. Behind it, she had already written on the chalkboard. MATH TEST, it said, followed by a happy face.

Derek groaned. He had completely forgotten there was a test today, and he hadn't studied. It sure seemed to him that they were having a lot more tests and exams than in grade five.

Oh well, he thought. How hard can this be?

Mrs. MacDonald walked up and down the rows, placing the tests face down as she talked away about what a nice morning it was, and how she hoped they were all looking forward to their Halloween dance.

"When I tell you to start, you can turn the papers over. You will have twenty minutes to complete the test. Your first instruction is to read over the entire test before beginning the questions. And I strongly suggest you do this."

She finished handing out the tests.

"You may begin now."

Derek tried to look at Ravine without being obvious. She was reading the test, and he saw her quickly flip to the second page. Derek decided he would never finish two pages of math problems in twenty minutes if he did this, so he ignored the first instruction and started answering the questions.

Twenty minutes seemed to go by quickly. It certainly wasn't enough time for Derek to answer all the questions on the test, but he got through most of them. He was good at math, so he was pretty sure he would get a good grade, or at least better than anyone else. Except Ravine, naturally.

The rest of the morning dragged on. History followed science, and by the time they took their books out for English, Derek was about ready for a nap. He usually liked schoolwork, but this morning seemed to be incredibly dull. By recess, he was pretty sure someone had added a few extra hours into the morning.

Derek had to go the bathroom before going outside, so by the time he got out to the yard his friends were already together and laughing about the math test.

As he approached them, Lisa was talking.

"It looked a lot harder because there were so many questions. Good thing we listened to Mrs. M. and read the whole thing first. Who knew you were only supposed to answer the odd numbered questions."

They all chuckled, and Derek laughed nervously. This was not going to be good.

When Ravine got home from school that afternoon, without Derek, she was in such a hurry she didn't even dump her backpack inside the front door, as she usually did. She ran upstairs to her room and hid herself away. Dumping all her stuff on the bed, she walked toward the mirror.

Abigail was smiling at her, as if she had been waiting. Ravine stretched out her hand to touch the smooth cold glass. With a sudden flash, she disappeared through the mirror.

Ravine was lying in a meadow, under a clear blue sky. It was warm, the sun was shining, and a girl was skipping around her in the grass.

"Come play with me," the girl said.

Ravine stood up slowly. She had a funny feeling deep in the pit of her stomach.

Abigail stopped skipping and stood still, looking at Ravine and smiling.

"Well, come on," she said again. "Don't just stand there."

Ravine looked around her. She could see a cabin a little distance up a gentle slope. The meadow they were in was really the back yard of the cabin.

She looked back at Abigail.

"Are you talking to me?" Ravine asked, unsure if the girl could see or hear her.

"Of course I'm talking to you," the girl said laughing. "Who else would I be talking to?"

Ravine looked around again. It was just the two of them. No one else was there.

She watched as Abigail started to skip around the yard again. The girl's long cotton skirt whisked around her calves as she twirled in circles. Her scuffed boots had definitely seen better days, and Ravine gazed at Abigail's worn skirt and blouse. They might even be hand-me-downs, she thought.

But despite the old grey skirt and blouse, a delicate silver chain with a heart-shaped locket hung around her neck. It shone brightly in the sun, seeming to be out of place with the girl's clothing.

The sun was feeling hotter, and Ravine realized she didn't need her heavy sweatshirt. She pulled it over her head and dropped it on the grass, still watching the girl.

"Why are you dressed like a boy?" Abigail asked, as she skipped closer.

Ravine looked at her torn jeans and pink t-shirt.

"I'm not dressed like a boy," she said defensively.

Abigail laughed. "Sure you are. Who ever heard of a girl wearing pants? And funny looking ones at that."

Ravine was about to answer when they heard a loud bang from the back door.

"Abigail!"

The same woman Ravine had seen in the cabin when she had first passed through the mirror was standing on the wooden porch.

"Yes, Mama?"

At least Ravine knew she was back at the same place as the last time she went through the mirror. But she still didn't know where that was. Or when.

The woman walked toward Abigail and stepped right through Ravine as if Ravine weren't there. Ravine's body tingled as her image briefly faded in and out of focus.

She was stunned and frightened. The woman had passed right through her like Ravine was a ghost.

And obviously, the woman wasn't deaf or blind.

"Abigail, you didn't do your chores, and Abe is going to be home any minute. Get inside the house and clean up. Supper's on."

"I'm sorry, Mama. I forgot." Abigail smiled.

"Yes, yes, I know," her mother said, gently. "And you forgot yesterday, and the day before and the day before…"

"And the day before that," Abigail laughed.

"Oh, Abigail, what are we going to do with you? You've always got your head in the clouds."

Ravine watched Abigail's mother put her arm around the girl as they turned and walked toward the cabin. Ravine could only barely hear the rest of their conversation as they walked up the steps to the porch.

Everything looked so real and solid to her, yet only the young girl seemed to be able to see her. She bent down to pick a daisy, but she could not grasp it. Her fingers passed right through, as if she were trying to pick up water. Bending down closer, though, she could smell its fragrance. This was strange. She was able to climb the ladder to the loft, and sit on the chair in the kitchen, and even feel the grass under her feet. But she could not pick a flower.

Ravine hurried to catch up to Abigail and her mother. The front door swung shut behind them just as Ravine got there. She tried knocking on the door, but her hand went through it, like her whole body had gone through the mirror.

She stepped back, staggered. What was going on? Where was she? Why could Abigail see her, and even talk to her, when her mother couldn't?

She sat on the front step in fear, thoughts whizzing through her brain as she tried to make some sense of all this. Her mind went back a few months, and she recalled Isabel Roberts, the ghost who lived at 56 Water Street. Isabel was able to pass through walls and doors as if they weren't there. Did that mean Ravine was a ghost?

No, she couldn't be a ghost. So she must be dreaming. A sudden chill swept through her body, even though the day was bright and warm.

After a while, she decided the only thing to do was to go inside and learn what she could. Ravine headed toward the door and instead of opening it, she simply walked through it like she would pass through a fog. She realized that even though everything appeared real, as if she belonged here, her invisibility or lack of a physical body, or whatever this was, meant this was not her world. She could move around in this world but not disturb anything, like open a door or pick a flower.

Everything seemed vaguely familiar, as though she somehow knew these people.

Once inside, Ravine found Abigail setting the table while her mother was removing a large pot from the hearth. She could smell the soup. It reminded her she was hungry.

"Didn't you say Abe was going to be home soon, mama?"

"Oh, he's been working at the Johnson's Farm and he said he wouldn't be late. So I'm sure he'll be here soon."

Ravine sat at the table beside Abigail. At first, the girl gave no indication that she knew Ravine was there. Abigail helped herself to a bowl and filled it with soup. When her mother wasn't looking, she turned to Ravine and smiled.

"Mama, can I read to the baby tonight?"

Her mother smiled and placed her hands on her stomach. Ravine hadn't noticed the roundness of her belly before, but she was obviously expecting a baby.

"Yes, Abigail. As soon as you get your chores done."

Ravine got up and climbed the ladder to Abigail's bedroom. She looked down from the loft and watched as the young girl ate her supper, and felt a sudden sadness wash over her. She wasn't sure how old Abigail was right now, but she did know that the girl was going to die soon, and there was absolutely nothing Ravine could do to change that.

Just then she heard the front door downstairs open and slam shut. She looked down into the kitchen to see a tall handsome man. He had a short beard, and he was dirty like he'd been working all day. He had a kindly face, and he was playfully ruffling Abigail's hair while he kissed her mama.

She looked around Abigail's bedroom, but there wasn't much to see. There were no books, games, or toys. A small bed, a dresser, and the mirror that brought Ravine to this world.

Ravine reached out to touch the mirror, and in a flash she was through it and gone.

Back in her room, Ravine heard a knock at her door.

Her mother turned the knob and slowly pushed it open, peeking inside. Ravine was lying on her bed with her eyes half closed.

"Were you sleeping?"

Ravine shook her head.

"What time is it?" she asked.

"It's dinner time. I think someone fell asleep."

Ravine shook her head again. But she felt as if she had been gone for hours. Or maybe days. She just couldn't tell. She knew she was tired, and she felt drained, as if she had just run a long distance.

And she was starving.

"What's for dinner?"

"Meatloaf."

Just before her mother turned to go, she stopped and turned around.

"That mirror is really too big for your bedroom, Ravine. I don't know what you find so attractive about it," she said, with a shrug.

Ravine turned to look at the mirror. Abigail smiled sweetly at her.

"There are some beautiful things about it, they're just hidden," Ravine said as she followed her mother and shut the door behind them.

The week went by slowly. Everyday, Ravine walked to and from school on the other side of the street, with her head down, ignoring Derek. At school, it was worse. In every class, their seats were either beside each other or one in front of the other. They ignored each other, but if they did happen to catch each other's eye, there was an exchange of dirty looks before they quickly turned away.

Their friends felt the tension too. But no one said anything about it.

It was hard hanging out with the group when Derek was around, so Ravine started bringing a book to school and she spent her recesses and lunchtime reading by herself.

"Are you mad at me?"

Ravine looked up to see Joannie standing in front of her.

"Of course not," Ravine replied.

"Are you mad at Derek?" Joannie asked. She sat down in a pile of leaves next to Ravine.

'Derek's mad at me," Ravine said, defensively.

"Oh. Well, that doesn't mean you can't hang with us, you know," Joannie said.

"Yes, I know," Ravine whispered.

Joannie sat with Ravine until the bell rang. As they were getting up to head inside, Derek and Sunil walked by.

"Yo! Ravine!" Sunil yelled and waved.

Derek didn't even look her way.

After school, Sunil and Joannie walked home together. They talked about Derek and Ravine.

"Ravine said Derek is mad at her."

"That's not what Derek says. He said she's mad at him," Sunil replied.

"When I asked her at recess if she was mad at him, I thought she was going to cry. She didn't, but I think it was close. She wouldn't talk about it, though. She just changed the subject and told me all about the book she's reading. If I hear anything more about this book, I won't ever have to read it myself."

"Derek won't say anything either. But he's been acting kinda strange for a few weeks now. And I think that started before anything happened between him and Ravine.

They continued on for a while in silence.

"What if they never make up?" Joannie asked. "Ravine and Derek never fight."

"They'll make up," Sunil said, trying to convince himself more than Joannie.

Thursday night.

It was late, and Ravine sat at her desk, bent over her schoolbooks. She had been so preoccupied with the mirror, she had almost forgotten about the history quiz in the morning.

She had been staring at the same page full of names and dates for quite a while, and nothing seemed to be sinking in. It was hard for her to ignore the mirror, and every time she caught a glimpse out of the corner of her eye, she knew Abigail would be there, smiling and waving. She was inviting Ravine to come back, and it was getting harder and harder to ignore her.

Finally, to distract herself, Ravine pushed her chair away from the desk and slowly walked around the room in small circles. She noticed the material for her Halloween costume crumpled up in a corner. She hadn't even started it. All she had at this point was a couple of lengths of grey, metallic material and an idea of what she wanted to do with it.

As she continued pacing, she looked toward

Abigail, back to her desk, and then back at the wrinkled material.

Reluctantly she walked to the shiny heap on the floor and sat down. Picking up a needle and thread, she pulled the material toward her. It was going to be a long night, she thought.

Ravine was still awake, her eyes only half opened. She couldn't stop yawning. Everyone else had gone to bed long ago, and all the lights in the house were off except in her room. From the street, someone passing by would have seen a single faint glow from a pink lampshade.

The clock on her night table said it was four in the morning.

Tired, but pleased, she held up her finished costume. She threw it back into the corner, leaving it once again in a crumpled heap. She was glad it was done, but her enthusiasm for the party was gone. She and Derek were supposed to be married monsters, and now they weren't even talking to each other.

Abigail was still smiling and waving at Ravine.

Despite the time, and how tired she felt, Ravine didn't hesitate. She extended her hand toward the smooth, cold glass. It bit into Ravine's arm like an icicle, and she was instantly sucked out of her own world and plunged into a white light. Briefly trapped, Ravine closed her eyes and waited to be swept to wherever Abigail was taking her. But passing between these worlds seemed to take a little longer than before, and she began to panic.

Suddenly, she landed on something soft.

Ravine opened her eyes and found herself in Abigail's room. The room was lit only slightly by a small oil lamp, and the rest of the cabin was dark. Abigail was sitting on the bed beside her, holding a picture.

"Who's that?"

"My papa."

Abigail did not look at Ravine when she responded, but continued staring at the small black and white photo.

"I thought Abe was your father," said Ravine. The man in the photo was definitely not Abe.

Abigail set the picture on her bed.

"Abe is my papa now because he married my mama," she said.

Ravine sat in silence, waiting for Abigail to continue.

"My real papa died a few years ago. He was thrown from his horse. My mama says that my papa is a star looking down on me." She stood up and opened the curtains. "That one, right there," she said, pointing to the brightest star in the sky.

Ravine nodded. "Sure, that's the North Star."

"Yes! That's my papa," she exclaimed. Then she sat back on the bed next to Ravine.

"Every night, I wait until I can see that star, and then I tell my papa everything about my day. But sometimes it's cloudy, and I have to wait for another night. If it's cloudy many nights in a row, by the time I get to talk to Papa I have a lot to tell him. I'm always sad on the cloudy nights."

Abigail fell silent.

"Papa went away when I was only little," she continued. "Sometimes I think he's coming back, only he never does. But I have his picture, and I can see his star in the sky, so I know everything is alright."

She took Ravine's hand, and Ravine felt a tingling sensation in her fingers. She was surprised Abigail was able to touch her since everything else she tried to touch went right through her.

"Do you like my mirror?" Abigail said suddenly. They stood up together and walked over to it.

"Yes. I like your mirror," Ravine said, her voice shaking.

"My papa gave it to me. He said the angel on

the top reminded him of me. He used to call me his little angel."

Ravine had never paid much attention to the carved angel on top of the frame until now. But Abigail was right; it did look a lot like her.

They stared at each other in the mirror.

"Why am I here, Abigail?"

"Because you want to be," she said. Her eyes bore into Ravine's.

Abigail was right. Ravine did want to be here to find out what happened to this girl. But she was sure it was Abigail who brought her here, not the other way around. Abigail needed her, only she probably didn't know that yet, and Ravine didn't know what she was needed for.

"Where is here, Abigail?"

"Well, here is right here, silly. We're right where we are. We couldn't be any place else, could we?"

She turned her back on the mirror and faced Abigail.

"How did you die?"

"I'm not dead," Abigail said. "You're not alive yet." She stood closer to Ravine.

"How come you can see me if I'm not alive yet?" Ravine asked.

"I can see lots of things other people can't see."

Abigail stepped closer to her, and Ravine

instinctively took a step backwards. Abigail said she was able to see spirits and see things that were unexplainable, just like she could. It was odd to think of herself as a spirit, but what else could she be? In Abigail's world, she wasn't even born yet.

Ravine's mind was spinning.

"How old are you, Abigail?"

"If you didn't want to be here you wouldn't be," Abigail said again. "I'm almost ten years-old."

From the dates on the tombstone, Ravine knew Abigail would soon die. As the girl took another step closer, Ravine took another backward step and fell into the depths of the mirror.

She landed softly on the floor in her own bedroom. Getting up, she looked around. Everything was the way she had left it. Her history book was still on her floor, still opened to the page she had not yet studied. Her pink lamp was still glowing softly, casting shadows around the room.

And there was a shimmer of light that seemed to come from within the mirror.

You're here because you want to be, Abigail had told her. And she was in the glass now, smiling.

Ravine stared.

"What's going on Abigail? What happened to you?"

Chapter 6

Derek woke the next morning to the shrill sound of his alarm. He rolled over and hit it with his fist, and then buried his head deep into his pillow. He was slowly falling back into a dreamy sleep when his mother barged into the room, flicked on the light, opened his curtain and pulled the covers from his head.

Without a word, she left and shut the door behind her.

Derek stretched his arms over his head slowly. Realizing that today was Friday, he jumped out of bed and got dressed quickly. Tonight was the Halloween party.

He picked up his costume and thought about Ravine. This should have been a great night, but if he was going to have to go to the party as only half of a couple, he would. I've got other friends, he thought. And I'm going to have fun.

He headed downstairs to the kitchen, jumping over the last three steps.

I've got other friends.

He sat at the table eating his cereal, listening to Danielle and his mom fight. Just like most other mornings.

"You're not wearing that!"

"Yes, I am! What's wrong with it?"

"It's quite simple," his mother began. "The skirt's too short and so is the top."

I've got other friends, Derek reminded himself again, as the fight continued. The night was going to be a scream! He finished his breakfast and interrupted the discussion to say goodbye.

"Have a good day, sweetheart," his mother said. Then she leaned over to give him a kiss. He glanced at Danielle, who was glaring at him, and turned to leave just as his sister and mother got back to their argument.

He slammed the front door behind him and walked down the steps. Still no change. There was Ravine walking quickly on the other side of the street with her head down.

He did have other friends.

Derek flung his backpack over his shoulder and started walking to school, without trying to catch up.

Alone.

He made sure to stomp on every pile of frost-covered leaves. When they crunched loudly under his shoes, he looked up to see if Ravine would react, but by now she was too far ahead of him.

Excitement filled the schoolyard. Everybody was anxious to impress their friends with their costumes.

In the classrooms, the teachers weren't having much luck keeping their pupils focused on schoolwork. Some of the kids had been selected weeks ago to be on the Halloween Party Committee, and those kids were excused from their classes before morning recess.

The Halloween committee spent most of the day getting everything ready for the big night. As Joannie, Lisa, Sunil, and Annie tested lights, others were setting up tables for the food and drinks. And there was one special table for the DJ to use for his equipment. The janitor was there to hang up the disco ball.

They made designs on bright orange Bristol board to decorate the walls.

"This Indian ink is really great stuff," said Annie.

"India ink."

"Huh?"

"It's called India ink," Sunil said. "You should trust me on this one. But that's not what this is anyway. This is just cheap black ink."

At lunchtime and afternoon recess, nobody was talking about anything except tonight's party. Even the history test that Ravine had not studied for was cancelled because the teacher knew no one was paying any attention.

When school was over, Ravine once again walked home on the other side of the street, leaving Derek alone. But he was determined not to let Ravine ruin this night for him.

He turned up his driveway and watched Ravine run up her front steps, shutting the door behind her. He opened his own front door and yelled, "I'm home!"

Ravine shut her bedroom door behind her. She immediately picked up her costume and held it in front of her, turning from side to side to see how she looked.

"What do you think, Abigail? Do you like it?"

Abigail smiled her sweet smile. She couldn't respond to Ravine through the mirror, but that didn't stop Ravine from talking to her anyway.

Ravine put on her costume, and decided she

looked great. Then she decided she wasn't going to the party, and undressed again. She got back into her ripped jeans and sweater and looked at Abigail.

Abigail smiled.

"You know how it is, don't you, Abigail? Life sucks when you're not talking to your best friend."

Abigail smiled.

"Would you go to the party if you were me?"

Abigail smiled.

"I didn't think so," Ravine said.

Abigail gestured to Ravine to follow her, and Ravine reached her hand through the mirror to grab Abigail's hand. With a flash, Ravine was gone.

Like the last time, Ravine felt as if she was being suspended in the whiteness longer before crossing into Abigail's world.

Ravine and Abigail walked hand in hand through a grassy meadow.

"Where are we going?" Ravine asked.

They reached the edge of the meadow, and continued down a steep slope where they crossed a narrow gravel road.

"To my favourite place in the whole wide world," Abigail announced. "Come on. Don't be a slowpoke."

Ravine ran to catch up to Abigail.

"Does your mother ever call you Abby?"

They were at the bottom of the hill now, approaching an old forest of very tall trees. The understory beneath the trees was not covered with bushes, and was open enough to walk through easily. There was a soft carpet of fallen leaves and pine needles that gave off a delightful smell.

"No, but my papa used to call me Abs. Abe called me that one time and I told mama to tell him not to. Sometimes Abe calls me Abby, but not often. My cousin Henry always calls me Abby."

"Is Henry related to your mama?"

"No, he's Abe's nephew. He's very different. His last name is Adams, just like my mama's name now. I have a few aunts and uncles on my papa's side, but I don't see them much anymore. Their last name is Baldwin, same as me."

As they entered the forest, Ravine commented that it smelled so nice in there. Abigail smiled.

"You have a different name. I have never heard of a name like that before," Abigail said.

Ravine nodded. "I was born out west, in a little town that didn't even have a thousand people."

"Gosh, that's a pretty big town, if I do say so," Abigail interrupted.

"Well, in the middle of this town was a ravine.

It ran from one end of the town to the other, and it was full of beautiful trees and flowers. And animals. Lots of deer, and rabbits, and skunks. And birds singing. It was my mom and dad's favourite place in the whole town, so when I was born they named me Ravine. We moved east shortly after I was born, so I haven't ever seen the ravine I was named after. Now, my father works in a big city, but we live in a small town nearby. The town is called Summerhill. My mother and father liked it because there's a pretty river that flows through the town, and it reminded them of the place back west where we were all born. "

"Do you have a pet name?"

Ravine shook her head. One time, way back in grade one, Derek called her Veeny. He never did it again after she threatened to beat him up. They were the same size back then, and he knew she could do it.

The girls were quiet for a little while as they continued deeper into the forest. It was peaceful and smelled fresh; the only sounds were their own footsteps on the soft carpet of fallen pine needles.

"Where are we going?" Ravine finally asked.

"Up here." Abigail pointed up a rocky hill. "I'm taking you to my very favourite place. Remember?"

And the two girls started to climb the hill, venturing deeper into the forest.

Derek stood beside King Tut, who was accompanied by an Egyptian mummy. In a dark gymnasium that was lit only by skeleton flashlights, the costumes looked fantastic. He could tell that King Tut must be Sunil, by his height and his darker skin colour. And he guessed that the mummy must be Joannie, because he knew that Sunil and Joannie were planning something together. He had to admit Sunil looked great.

As far as he knew, no one had recognized him yet. His Frankenstein costume included a lot of makeup and a kind of hat he had made, to hold electrodes and to disguise the shape of his head. Plus he was wearing shoes that made him even taller than before. He knew that everyone would recognize him once he located Ravine, because they were always together.

But where was Ravine? He looked around the room but couldn't see her anywhere. So he wandered through the crowd, thinking he must have just missed her.

Soon the gym began to fill, but there was still no Ravine.

He saw Annie and Lisa walking toward him.

They looked really good. Annie had tied back her long red hair with what looked like seaweed, and a sparkling green mermaid tail dragged behind her. Derek thought immediately of the Little Mermaid, and he expected Annie to start singing the Mermaid song at any moment.

Lisa was a cowgirl. She was wearing a big cowboy hat that almost hid her face, cowboy boots, and a short hoop skirt. She carried a lasso over her shoulder.

"Hi, Derek. Where's Ravine?"

"Haven't seen her," he replied. So much for my clever makeup, he thought.

The music suddenly boomed through the gym and the disco ball lit up. Silver confetti lights whirled around the walls and all the fairy tale characters, movie stars, rock stars, monsters, and mermaids cheered loudly. King Tut raised his wand and bowed, as if trying to take credit for all the lights and music.

The dance floor was filled with ghosts and goblins, vampires and wizards, cowboys and cowgirls, fairy tale characters, and a lot of costumes from everybody's favourite movies. But there was no Bride of Frankenstein.

Derek walked around the outside of the dance floor, wondering what had happened to Ravine.

He knew she was mad at him, but this wasn't like Ravine. She always kept her promises. About an hour after the beginning of the dance, he knew for sure she wasn't coming.

He left the gym and walked out into the cool, crisp night. A brisk October wind swept against his silver metallic face, and made his costume ruffle with a crinkly noise.

He was feeling uneasy about Ravine, so he walked quickly toward her house. As he hurried along, he passed a lot of startled people. One mother, out with her two small children, took shelter in a doorway when the kids started crying. Derek didn't stop to reassure them it was only a costume.

The wind cut through Derek's costume and he exhaled deeply. His breath turned to frost in the chilly air.

As he reached Ravine's house, he started to climb the stairs. But the extra high shoes he was wearing made him stumble, and he fell face first onto the front porch. Getting himself back up, he was just about to ring the doorbell when Ravine's mother looked out through the small glass window in the door. Even though it was not late, she was already in her slippers and long flannel nightgown. She fiddled with the lock.

"I thought I heard some noise out here. If I had

known it was a monster, I would have run away to hide."

"Hi, Mrs. Crawl. Where's Ravine?"

"Oh, didn't she call you? It's nothing to worry about," Mrs. Crawl began. "She wasn't feeling too well after supper, so she decided to stay home tonight."

"I'm sure she did call. But I was probably at Sunil's helping him with his costume. Can I go see her?"

Mrs. Crawl opened the door wider to let Derek in.

"Just let yourself out," she said, heading back into the family room. "Try not to fall again."

Derek poked his head into the family room. Mrs. Crawl had already settled down with her book, and Ravine's father was staring at the television. He probably hadn't heard Derek fall, and probably didn't even realize Ravine's mother had gotten up to let him in. He looked like he was glued to the set.

Derek climbed the stairs slowly. And more carefully.

He paused at Ravine's closed bedroom, and then slowly turned the knob and inched open the door. He closed it behind him and felt around for the light switch, standing completely still before turning it on.

Derek flicked the switch.

His eyes settled first on the big ugly mirror leaning against Ravine's wall. It looked completely out of place in this room.

But what really caught his attention was the fact he was alone. Where was Ravine?

He was sure she hadn't gone out, because the only way downstairs takes you right past the family room. Her parents would have seen her, even if she were trying to be quiet.

"Ravine? Are you here?"

No answer. But he thought, as he whispered his question, that a faint glow had appeared in the mirror.

Moving closer to the mirror, he gazed mechanically at his own reflection, then put his hand on the cold glass. Quickly, he drew his hand back. The glass felt cold, and there was also a slight electrical sensation. He thought his hand was a little red, and it tingled.

Derek knew this mirror had something to do with Ravine's disappearance. She had told him there was something strange about the mirror. She said there was a reflection from the other side of the mirror that wasn't her.

He spoke a little louder this time, and directly at the mirror.

"Where are you, Ravine? Are you in there?"

Still no answer, but the mirror began to glow brighter. He felt strangely attracted to it, and despite his experience just a moment ago, he reached out to touch it again. He spread out his fingers as he touched the cold glass and leaned against it.

A halo of light appeared instantly around the mirror. Temporarily blinded by the brightness and jolted by a surge of electricity, Derek stumbled and fell to the floor. Almost as quickly, the halo faded. As it did, the reflection Derek could see in the mirror was no longer his own. It was the young girl with the champagne hair.

Derek's eyes widened in disbelief. Ravine tried to tell him she was being haunted by this reflection, an image from the mirror that was not her own image. But he had pushed her away.

He stood up slowly, trying hard to regain his composure. The girl with the beautiful hair and innocent blue eyes smiled sweetly at him. He stared at her image, transfixed. Impulsively, he reached out to touch her.

His hand melted into the cold glass. His whole

body was being pulled into the glowing mirror. He tried to pull away, but the force was too strong. Scared, he surrendered to his fate.

Derek felt something like an invisible hand pulling him. Everything around him was white, like he was in the middle of a big cloud. But there was nothing solid, just white light.

Then, after what seemed like a few minutes, the brightness quickly disappeared and he was surrounded by total black. He landed softly on something prickly.

Opening his eyes, Derek found himself lying on a low bush beside a path, deep within a thick forest. He was covered with pine needles.

He stood up quickly and brushed himself off.

"Ravine!" he yelled, cupping his hands close to his mouth. But his voice came out as only a hoarse whisper.

Derek looked around. The forest undergrowth was sparse, so he could see a good distance through the trees. In spots, he could see the sun was shining brightly, but in most places, the tall trees cast dark shadows.

He didn't know which way to go, but he picked the uphill direction, thinking he might get to a higher spot where he could see around him. He started to walk aimlessly up the path, and kept trying to call out to Ravine. But his voice failed him. He tried clearing his throat, but that didn't help. He noticed his breathing was quick and shallow, even though he was walking slowly. The air seemed quite thin under the trees, and it was warm.

Derek did not know where he was. The forest had a feeling of vague familiarity, but it was nothing he could identify.

He tried yelling again.

"Ravine!"

Almost no sound came out. Then he tried whispering.

"Ravine, where are you?"

That came out clear, but it was too quiet to travel very far. If she were close enough to hear that, she would have heard him scuffling through the pinecones.

His legs were trembling and sweat was forming on his forehead as he stumbled over tree roots and fallen branches. He walked further into the forest.

It dawned on him that part of the reason it felt so warm in here was that he was still dressed as Frankenstein, complete with all his make-up. The metallic face paint was beginning to trickle down his cheeks as he sweated more. Even though he was lost and afraid, he chuckled to think someone would get an awful fright if they came upon him in these woods.

The trees lined up like tall soldiers along the sides of the path. He wondered who made the path. It didn't look like it was well travelled, but it was obviously not just a natural feature. A few times, a squirrel or chipmunk darted across the path, scurrying under the brush or up a tree. But he could hear no birds.

A soft breeze through the trees created strange noises that made the hair on the back of his neck stand on end.

As he walked further, he thought he could hear voices.

The voices sounded as if they were coming from somewhere close by, but sound in the forest was deceptive, and he couldn't tell how near the voices were, or in which direction. He stood still listening. The voices belonged to girls, and there were at least two of them.

The sounds were muffled by all the trees, but he finally decided the direction he thought they were most likely coming from. He stepped off the path and headed in that direction. As he started to make his way through the trees, the girls' voices seemed to be getting louder. At least he had guessed the right way.

Then he heard clearly, "Where are we going?"

It was Ravine's voice.

Derek ran further into the forest, pushing through tree branches and stumbling over roots. He cut his cheek on one branch, but didn't notice it. The louder the voices became, the faster he ran. As he drove deeper into the forest, he realized that he was climbing higher and further from the path. At this point there was no turning back, and he knew he was lost.

"Ravine," he tried to call out, cupping his hands around his mouth. He stopped to listen. Silence. In the thick trees, his voice died and fell to the forest floor.

He continued through the trees, and further up the hill. Then he heard Ravine yelling in the distance, but she seemed to be further away now.

"Wait up, Abigail!"

Excited by the sound of her voice, Derek broke into a run. He didn't get very far before he caught his toe on a tree root and lost his footing. As he stumbled forward, he came to the edge of a steep cliff, and disappeared over the side.

For some reason, Derek didn't feel frightened. The fall seemed to go on for a long while, but when he finally hit bottom, it was a soft landing.

Opening his eyes, he found himself back in Ravine's room, lying on her bed.

He could still hear Ravine's mother talking downstairs, and the sound of the television. Looking at the clock on Ravine's night table, he was pretty sure no time had passed. He had no idea where he had been, but wherever it was, Ravine was still there.

Standing up, he gazed into the mirror. It was just himself looking back. But his make-up had run all down his face with the sweat, and he had a cut on his cheek. At least that part was real, he thought.

Derek backed away from the mirror and left quickly, closing the door behind him. He hurried down the stairs and waved goodbye.

"Ravine's feeling better," he said. "But she's tired, and she told me to let you know she's going to sleep."

He slammed the door behind him as he left.

Ravine's father looked up from the television. "Was that Derek?" he asked.

"Abigail! Wait up, you're going too fast!"

Ravine pushed the tree limbs out of her way and tried to catch up, but now Abigail was out of sight.

"Abigail! Slow down!"

But Abigail was gone.

Ravine panicked, and began to hurry. She ran as fast as she could, pushing past the branches. Pine needles poked at her face and hands. As she moved through the forest, she knew she was lost.

At last she came to a break in the trees, where the forest suddenly ended. She was atop a high cliff, and she quickly backed away from the edge. She shivered as she looked down, seeing the dangerous drop to a river that flowed at the bottom. As far as she could see in the distance, there was nothing but trees. They were everywhere, although she could make out the winding path the river followed as it cut through the forest.

Lost or not, she couldn't help being amazed at what she saw. This was the most breathtaking view she had ever seen. It seemed vaguely familiar, but she knew she could never have been here before. From this height she couldn't be sure, but it looked as if the river flowed swiftly.

She was so busy staring at the scenery that she didn't hear when Abigail came up behind her.

"Boo!"

Startled, Ravine turned around quickly to find Abigail behind her, grinning.

"That wasn't funny, you know," she said with a frown. "I could have fallen."

Abigail picked up a stone and threw it off the

side of the cliff. They watched as it fell, finally making a small splash in the water below. Although it must have made a sound too, they couldn't hear it so far up.

"It sure is a long way down," Ravine said, as she backed away from the edge.

Abigail sat down and let her legs dangle off the side.

"It sure is" she replied. "This is my favourite place in the whole world."

Ravine nodded. She could understand why, but she was always uneasy with heights, and this one was making her feel more queasy than usual. One slip and …

"We better head back," Ravine said. She tried to sound calm. "It's getting dark."

Abigail finally stood up slowly, standing very close to the edge. She kicked a few pebbles into the empty space, and watched as they tumbled to the bottom.

"Come on, Abigail," Ravine said uneasily. "You're standing too close. You could fall."

"Like this?" Abigail pretended to fall, leaning from side to side. She stretched her arms out like she was walking a tightrope.

She laughed. "Does this make you nervous, Ravine?"

"It's not funny, Abigail. Come down, before something bad happens."

Abigail backed away from the edge, and came to Ravine and hugged her.

"Nothing bad is going to happen. I've been up here hundreds of times. Sometimes, I even come up here with Gent."

Ravine took Abigail's hand and began leading the way back down the path, and far from the edge of the cliff.

"Who's Gent?"

"My horse," Abigail replied. "He's beautiful."

The sun was beginning to set when Abigail's mother stepped out onto the back porch.

"Abigail!" she called, looking around the yard. "Abigail!"

Abe and Henry emerged from the barn.

"Is Abigail with you?" Meredith called to them.

Henry shook his head.

"No, I haven't seen her," Abe replied.

Abe and Henry walked toward the house.

"Abigail," her mother called again. "Oh, where is that girl. She knows I don't like it when she's out so late."

"Abigail!"

"I'm sure she's alright, Meredith," Abe said gently. "She probably just went into the forest."

He turned to look toward the forest. "Look, here she comes now."

Abigail and Ravine emerged from the forest and crossed the wide space leading to the house. Henry went inside while Abe and Meredith waited for Abigail to get to the house.

"I told you not to go into the forest," Meredith said sternly.

Abigail laughed.

"No, mama. You said you didn't want me to go in the forest when it got dark. It won't be dark for at least another hour."

But she could see the strain on her mother's face.

"I'm fine, mama. Really, I am."

Ravine followed Abigail into the house and up the ladder. They stood in front of the mirror.

"Good night, Abigail."

Ravine pushed hard against the glass, and in a few seconds she was gone. When she opened her eyes, she was sitting on the floor in her own room. She took a deep breath and looked at Abigail in the mirror, smiling and waving at her. She gazed until the reflection faded and only her own image remained, then inched away from the mirror.

Derek walked home in silence. Ravine was right. She wasn't normal, and neither was he. And he wasn't happy about that. But he was beginning to realize there was nothing he could do about it. Still, if there was any way to avoid doing things that were abnormal, he was sure going to try.

He opened the front door and kept his head down.

"Hi, Mom."

"You're home early," she said.

"Probably couldn't get any girls to dance with him," Danielle snorted. "Maybe you should give them money, so they'll pretend to like you." She laughed, then stuck her tongue out at him.

"That's quite enough, Danielle," their mother said.

Derek didn't comment. He just wanted to get upstairs and get out of his Frankenstein costume.

Walking up the stairs, he realized his legs were aching. As he removed his costume, he could see his knees were starting to bruise from where he fell in the forest. And he still had the scratch on his face. He was glad his mother hadn't asked how he got it.

As he finished getting out of the costume and into his pajamas, he kept thinking about Ravine.

Where was she? He knew she was in the mirror somewhere, but he didn't have any idea where that was.

Looking in his own mirror, he began to clean off the rest of his make-up. He looked at himself, grateful that he was seeing his own reflection. But he kept thinking about the reflection that stared back at him when he looked into the mirror in Ravine's room. He wondered if the other voice he heard in the forest was the girl with the champagne hair.

When he was finally cleaned up, he went to his window and pushed back the curtain. There was still a light shining in the construction site across the street, and he could see the night watchman leaning against a shed, smoking his pipe.

He turned quickly, suddenly sensing that someone was there with him.

But no hand touched his shoulder.

No chills ran up his spine.

At last, he closed the curtains and flopped on his bed, talking out loud to himself.

"Who wants to be normal, anyway?"

He crossed his arms over his chest, and closed his eyes.

A girl's voice whispered softly in his ear, "Nobody, Derek. Nobody."

Chapter 7

"What do you think?"

Ravine and Derek sat on her bed staring at each other. She was relieved when he had knocked on her door this morning. He didn't call before he came over, and her mother had just sent him upstairs. He had knocked on her door, and let himself into her room without waiting for her to answer.

"I believe you," he said. "I always believed you. I just didn't want to get involved in another one of these mysteries. Then I guess I was mad when you could see the girl in the mirror and I couldn't."

Ravine looked at him in silence. This was completely unexpected.

Derek continued. "I've told you before that I don't want any of this spooky stuff, that I just want to be normal like the other kids."

He looked at her, but she waited quietly for him to go on.

"But last night, I realized it isn't my choice. I'm weird. We're both weird, and there's nothing we can do about it. So, I'm sorry. Okay?"

They stared at each other for a few seconds.

"Sure, yeah," Ravine stuttered. "No problem."

They remained silent for a few minutes.

"I missed you," Ravine said. "I know you don't like the spooky stuff, but I could always count on you. It's more than that. Something is bugging you, I can tell. What's up?"

Derek didn't answer.

"So, tell me about the possessed mirror and the girl in it," he finally said. "I finally saw her when I came here last night looking for you."

Ravine was delighted, but she tried not to show it. She shook her head.

"Not until you tell me what's going on with you lately. Something's up, and I want to know what it is." She stared at Derek.

He broke the gaze and focused on a rip in the knee of his jeans. He stuck his finger in it and pulled. The sound of denim ripping could be heard throughout the room.

"It's probably nothing, so don't worry about it, okay?"

Of course it was something.

"No, it's not okay. We've always leveled with

each other about everything. Tell me, or I won't tell you about Abigail."

After a few moments of silence, Derek looked up and rolled his eyes.

"Oh, fine!" he said. "There's weird stuff going on with my mom, and I think it has something to do with me."

"Go on," Ravine coaxed.

"Well, it seems like every time she gets a phone call, she starts to whisper. Then when she sees me, she hangs up quickly. When I ask who she was talking to, she always just brushes me off with some excuse. It's been going on for a couple of weeks now, and it's kinda freaking me out. She's hiding something."

"Yeah, that does seem weird. Do you know who she's talking to?"

Derek shook his head. "No idea. But I can tell it has something to do with me. I think she must be talking to the same person every time, but I don't know for sure. She sounds nervous and annoyed during those calls, too."

"Have you asked Danielle if she knows anything about this?"

"As if she's going to talk to me about anything," Derek snorted.

"Is there anything I can do to help?"

Derek shook his head. "I don't think so."

He paused.

"So now it's your turn. What's with the girl in the mirror?"

Ravine wanted to keep questioning Derek about the mysterious phone calls, but she could see he was agitated and she decided to let it go for now.

"Well, I don't know much," Ravine began.

Then she told him everything she could remember from the time she first set eyes on the mirror in Onna's shop. She told him how she felt an attraction to it that was hard to explain, and that she could see a glow coming from it that Onna didn't seem to notice. He already knew that when she looked into the mirror somebody else was looking back, at least some times.

"At first, the girl just smiled at me. Sometimes she waved, but then she started to wave at me to come toward her. I was very surprised when I touched the mirror and my hand went right into it like water."

She looked at Derek. No reaction.

"The next time I put my hand into the mirror, my whole body went in and I found myself in some strange house. That happened a few more times before I finally realized that I was going back in time. But I don't know where I travel to."

Derek nodded.

"Finally, I met the girl. The same mirror is in her room. Not a mirror just like mine, but the same one. This one. Derek, it's Abigail Baldwin. Remember her from the cemetery? She told me she is ten years-old, and we know Abigail died when she was ten. So I know what year I have been travelling to, and I know she is going to be dead soon."

"I guess that was her voice I heard talking with you in the forest," Derek said.

"What?!? What are you talking about?"

"I came over to your house last night, because you didn't show up for the dance. I ended up going through the mirror myself. I ended up in a forest, still dressed like Frankenstein, and I could hear you and another girl talking somewhere through the trees. I called out to you, but you didn't answer. Then I tripped, and fell off a cliff. When I opened my eyes, I was back here in your room. It didn't seem like time had passed at all."

He paused to let all this sink in.

"What do you think she wants?"

"I have no idea yet," said Ravine. "We don't know what happened to her all those years ago. But whatever it was, it's going to happen soon."

They sat quietly together, going over the story again. Derek was particularly interested in what

Onna might have told Ravine about the mirror. Ravine didn't think Onna had said anything important, but Derek was sure she must have.

"Didn't she say the mirror came from the old Baldwin property? And didn't she say it sort of appeared out of nowhere?"

"Yes."

"Well, c'mon, Ravine. Don't we know enough yet to realize that somebody, probably Abigail, is trying to contact us? To get us to help, or something? This wouldn't be the first time, would it?"

Ravine nodded.

"I think you're right, Derek. We better go see Onna to see if she knows anything more about the Baldwin family. She might not, but it's worth a try."

"What about the house where they found the mirror? Did Onna tell you where it is?"

Ravine shook her head.

"I bet it's Abigail's house," Derek said. "It just makes sense. We know the Baldwins lived around here, because Abigail is buried in our cemetery. We know the mirror came from some old house to your house, and that the same mirror is back in time in Abigail's house."

Ravine looked at Derek. He really could think logically.

"We've got to find out where that house is," she said, "to see if it will give us any clues."

Derek groaned. But he knew he didn't have much choice.

It was a beautiful day for a walk. The sun was low in the sky, but very bright. It was uncommonly warm for late October.

Derek and Ravine walked to *Maybe Antiques* that afternoon. Along the way, they went over again everything that they knew so far.

As they climbed the stairs to the shop, Ravine put her hand on Derek's arm.

"I better warn you. Onna likes to talk and talk. Sometimes you have to interrupt to get her back on track."

Ravine opened the door, and the little bell tinkled above their heads. Derek had only been here once before, and that was a couple years ago when Ollie was alive. His mother used to come here sometimes, but since Oliver's death, she didn't stop in here anymore. He couldn't remember if he saw Onna that one time.

"Hi, Ravine," Onna called out.

As soon as he saw the way Onna was dressed, Derek remembered her.

Onna glided over to greet them, her long skirt

flowing behind her. The skirt was decorated with strings of beads, and the row along the hem clattered against the floor as she walked. She was wearing another string of beads around her neck and a tie-dye blouse that looked like a sunburst. It sort of matched the blue skirt, but not much would have gone with the Kelly green running shoes. Onna had tied her long grey hair back today, to show off her large hoop earrings.

Ravine introduced Derek and Onna took his hand in hers, digging into him with her long colourful nails.

"It is so nice to meet you, Derek. Ravine talks about you all the time," Onna said with enthusiasm.

Derek nodded sheepishly, and looked at Ravine.

"Really? What does she say?"

He looked at Ravine again, but she turned away quickly.

"Well, she --"

Ravine interrupted.

"Onna, we came here to find out more about that house you were telling me about. You know, where they found that mirror I bought."

Onna let go of Derek's hand. "What house was that dear?"

"Remember? Before I bought the mirror, you were telling me all about how the Baldwins had found the mirror in the old house they were selling. We were wondering if you could tell us what street it was on."

Ravine looked at Derek. He was grinning at her, and she turned away again, blushing.

"Oh, and how is your mirror? Are you enjoying it, dear?"

Onna turned to Derek, without waiting for an answer. "Did Ravine tell you that when I was a little girl I had a mirror just like the one she bought? Oh, it was my favourite mirror ever. Some days I would spend my entire morning polishing the frame. My, my, that was a long time ago. I couldn't have been more than ten or eleven years-old, about the same age you two are now. Time does go by so quickly, you know. Sometimes I can't believe how the years have flown. Once --"

"Where did the mirror come from?" Ravine interrupted.

"Oh, it came from the old Baldwin place," Onna sniffed. "Like I told you. Not my mirror, not the one I had when I was little. I mean the one you bought."

Just then, they heard the bell above the door, and Onna went to greet the new customers.

"It just might take all day to get anything out of her," Derek whispered.

"Yeah. I told you she likes to talk."

"That's more than just talking," he said.

"Yeah, I know," Ravine laughed.

When the two new customers finally managed to slip away from Onna's chatter to look around the store by themselves, Derek and Ravine tried again.

"Where is the Baldwin House?" Derek asked as he approached Onna.

"Oh, it's out by that horse farm just outside of town. You know, the one where they have that big pumpkin patch and the maze every Halloween. And Halloween is just tomorrow, isn't it? My, the summer went by so fast, and pretty soon it's going to be winter. The horse farm is a beautiful bit of property, I must say. I always told Oliver I wanted to live on a farm. I wanted a few horses, some cows, and maybe even a rooster ..."

"A rooster? Why would you want a rooster?" asked Derek.

"Oh, I think that would be such a lovely way to wake up in the morning. A big old rooster letting you know it's time to start your day."

Ravine shook her head in frustration. But Derek seemed to be interested. Of course he would, she thought. There's hardly anything he hates as much as the shrill sound of an alarm clock in the morning.

"I don't think I know that place," Ravine said, trying to get both of them back on track.

"I do. My mom took Danielle and me there a couple of years ago to get a pumpkin and some homemade pies. Danielle complained the whole time."

"Danielle complains about everything, Derek."

"Well, if you keep going until where you see the horses," said Onna, "there is a long dirt path on the opposite side of the road. It's the shortcut to the farm, but you can't drive a car on it because it's too narrow. You could ride a bike on it, though. Anyway, if you take the path, eventually you come to a clearing where you'll see some hills. The house is just past the first hill. Or I guess you could get a canoe and take it to the Summerhill Park. Then you could follow Maplewood River, and it would lead you right to the old Baldwin place. 'Course, I'm not very good with things like north and south, so I'm not sure which way you would have to paddle the canoe. But it's in the same direction as the big cliff that looks down on the river."

"How do you know about the shortcut, Onna?" Derek asked.

"Oh heavens! When I was younger, we used to ride our bikes out there, me and my brother, to go walking in the woods. There's another little stream that meets the river there, and Donnie used to bring his fishing pole to catch carp and catfish in the stream."

"Who's Donnie?" Derek asked.

Ravine pulled on his sleeve.

"We've got to go, Onna. See you later. Thanks!"

And with another tug on his sleeve, Ravine pulled Derek out of the shop.

"So who's Donnie?"

Ravine sighed. "Oh for crying out loud, Derek!"

"What? I was just curious!"

"Her brother! If I hadn't pulled you away we would have been there all day!"

They headed home in silence.

"I like Onna," Derek said after a couple of blocks.

"This is going to be a long ride, isn't it? How long do you think it'll take to get there?"

They were almost home, and were trying to decide whether they really knew where they were going.

"Well, my guess is that it's about twenty minutes past the cemetery," said Derek. "So that means about an hour to get there. If we pedal fast. And if we aren't riding against the wind."

They watched the red and orange leaves swirl down the street. There was obviously a wind to worry about, but the way the leaves were swirling made it impossible to tell which way it was blowing.

"But," Derek continued, "if we're riding with the wind, we should make it there in less time."

They continued the rest of the way home in silence. Ravine stomped on as many leaves as she could, and avoided looking at Derek. He stole a few sideway glances at her.

Even though it was still fairly warm, it was getting colder each night, and it wouldn't be long before the first snowfall. They agreed that if they didn't go to the house today, they might not have another opportunity.

As they reached Derek's driveway, Ravine continued on home to get her bike.

"I'll be right back," she called, as she stepped onto her front lawn.

"Ravine?"

She turned around.

"So what did you say to Onna about me?"

Ravine just shrugged her shoulders, and turned away to hide her red face.

"Hey, I was just asking …"

The ride to the old Baldwin place didn't take as long as they expected. The wind was at their backs, and it had turned into a brisk breeze. So it pushed them along like two giant hands guiding them along the streets and winding hills.

Finding the horse farm with the pumpkin patch was easy. But the narrow path that led to the old house was a little tougher to locate. It had been a long time since anyone had come this way, and the path was overgrown with weeds. At first, they didn't even realize it was a path.

Onna was right, though. They would definitely have to ride single file, and even at the beginning of the path they could see it wouldn't be an easy ride. Roots jutted out from the ground, and in some places the path almost disappeared beneath shrubs and weeds. Derek and Ravine were forced to stop several times to walk their bikes.

None of this was familiar to either of them, and a couple of times they stopped to look at each other as though not sure they should go on.

But as they alternately walked and rode, the trees gradually became thicker and taller. The path was leading uphill into the forest, and the towering trees blocked out the sun, making it appear later than it already was.

Derek stopped.

"This is the place," he exclaimed.

Ravine was ahead of him. She stopped and turned around.

"What place?"

"This is the place I travelled to last night, when I went through the mirror." He looked all around him. "This is it. This is where I was. I know it is."

They stared at one another.

"You were here too, weren't you, Ravine? This is where I was when I heard you and the other girl. There should be a tall cliff up at the top of this hill, the one I fell off. On the left side, I think. And remember, Onna said there is a cliff around here somewhere."

They stood in silence for a couple of minutes looking all around them.

"Come on, Derek. Let's keep going."

Just ahead of them, they saw a clearing. Then, as if someone opened a gate, the forest unfolded into a meadow with a creek running along one side, at the edge of the trees.

"Onna said, follow the creek that runs into Maplewood River. This must be it," Ravine said.

"I'm pretty sure that the river and the park are over in that direction, and that's where this creek seems to be headed."

They stood side by side holding their bikes.

"Well, what are we waiting for? Let's go," she said.

They followed the creek around a clump of bushes, and suddenly they came to an old house.

"There it is! That's the house I visit when I come through the mirror. Abigail's house."

"Are you sure?" asked Derek.

"Oh, yes."

They stood at the bottom of a low hill, looking up at the back of the old house. They could see it had originally been not much bigger than a shack, but later someone had built an addition on to one side. They dropped their bikes and walked the rest of the way.

This was definitely the place. Ravine recognized it, even though the house had become more run down with time. She had only seen it as it looked more than a hundred years ago, without the addition.

The yard was mostly overgrown with weeds and creeping shrubs. The barn was gone, but you could still see the foundation where it used to stand. Everything else looked the same.

They walked up the rickety porch. The glass on the door was broken, and the late autumn wind blew around the jagged pieces, echoing inside the house. Derek tried the door handle but it wouldn't budge. He tried to push it open with his weight, but still the door remained securely shut.

"Let's walk around," Ravine said, "there's another door that leads into the kitchen."

It was the same with the back door. The handle wouldn't move, and they couldn't push the door open. Disappointed, they stepped down from the porch, wondering what to do.

Ravine looked at the back door again and noticed something that wasn't there when she visited Abigail.

"Look, Derek." She pointed to the bottom of the door. "Doesn't that look like one of those dog doors? Maybe we could get in that way."

They raced back up the steps. Derek was the first to reach it, and he pushed at the little door.

"Come on!" he said. "It looks like it was made for a pretty big dog. If I can't slide through it, you probably can. Then you can open the door from the inside."

It wasn't quite big enough for Derek to use, but Ravine was smaller and more agile. Even so, she had to squeeze to get in. She quickly unfastened the door for Derek. They let the door bang shut behind them.

"Wow!" Ravine said, looking around the kitchen. It had changed over the years. The long wooden table and the shabby chairs were gone, and so was the big old wood-burning stove. The wooden floor Ravine had seen was now replaced, or at least covered with linoleum. The bedroom had a shaggy carpet, with a few bare spots and stains. The carpet had to be just about the ugliest colour either of them had ever seen.

"Did people really buy carpet that looked like this?"

"I know. It's really gross. It kinda looks like a newborn baby's poop," said Ravine.

"That's gross."

"Yeah, but it isn't any more gross than this carpet. I mean, look at it."

The house was wired for electricity now, and there were a couple of broken light fixtures hanging from the ceiling. But with nobody living here anymore, the power was off.

"Let's check out Abigail's room."

They climbed the ladder leading to the loft.

"There's nothing up here," Derek said when he got to the top.

Ravine frowned. The room was completely

empty. It was as if Abigail had never existed in this room. Ravine looked toward the window. Outside was a tall tree. It can't be the same one as when Abigail was still alive, she thought. She was pretty sure that tree was already starting to rot way back then. But it looked like the same kind of tree, only much bigger. For some reason, the tree comforted her.

She looked through the window at the sky and, even though it was the middle of the afternoon, she thought could see the North Star. Beside it, Ravine was sure she could see a small glimmer like that of another star.

"Abigail," she whispered.

There wasn't anything else to see here, so they headed back down the ladder and out the door. They locked the kitchen door behind them, knowing they could get back in through the pet door.

Outside, they walked around aimlessly for a bit, not really sure if they had learned much or what they should do next.

Then Ravine stopped and yelled, "Abigail!"

Derek looked at her as she started to call out again.

"What are you doing? Are you nuts? Someone's going to hear you," said Derek. "We're on somebody else's property, you know."

"And who's going to hear me? No one lives here anymore, Derek."

When he didn't answer, she called out to Abigail again. There was no response from anyone, and there was no Abigail.

"Why do you think she is not showing herself? Do you think we can only be in her world if we go through the mirror?"

Derek shrugged. "I don't know. This whole thing is weird. And this place creeps me out. Like somebody is watching us."

Ravine felt it too. She was familiar with the feeling of invisible eyes on her, and she knew Derek was right. Somebody was watching them.

The ride home was tiresome. Even though the wind had died down completely, most of the ride was uphill. They didn't talk on the way, each of them lost in their thoughts about Abigail and the rundown house. And the mirror.

When they finally parted at Derek's driveway, Ravine waved goodbye.

"Oh, and by the way," she said, "you're just as weird as I am."

When Ravine climbed into bed that night, she left her night table light on. She stared at Abigail for a long time. The girl's image was in the mirror, smiling, but she wasn't waving.

Ravine was very confused. She learned last summer that there are ghosts. And she could see them, or least one of them. She learned that spirits or ghosts – she didn't really know what to call them – thought of her as somebody who could help them. Now she was learning she could pass through solid objects, and that she could travel back in time.

She was realizing that there were many strange and unexplained things in this world, that it was far more wondrous than she had ever imagined. And it seemed like the strangeness only showed itself to selected people. Like her and Derek. If she was weird, she was glad Derek was too. She didn't know how she could possibly stand it if he wasn't.

Even though Abigail had told her that Ravine had made the decision herself to travel back in time, she wasn't sure that was right. She thought Abigail must be summoning her for something, like Isabel had done in the house across the road.

Was going through the mirror the only way to go back in time? Could she also travel to the future?

And why was she seeing Abigail? She remembered clearly that she and Derek had stopped at Abigail's headstone when they first went to the cemetery looking for Isabel's grave. Why did that one attract their attention out of so many? It didn't look like anything special. But they had lingered over it, and wondered how this young girl had died, and whether she was related to the Baldwins that lived on the street next to theirs. Onna had spoken about Mr. Baldwin as if everyone would know who he was.

She didn't know the Baldwin family who owned the cabin where her mirror came from, or even if they were the same Baldwins who lived on the next street over.

She was getting sleepy, but just as she was about to drift off to sleep, her eyes shot open and she sat up straight.

Abigail is going to die soon, she thought. Am I supposed to change the past so that she doesn't? No, that can't be. If I change the past, the past wouldn't have happened, and Abigail's grave wouldn't be there with those dates on it. Sure, she would have died eventually, but not at age ten.

No, it can't be that someone wants me to change the past. Then what is this all about?

As all these ideas whizzed about in her brain, she desperately wanted to talk to her parents. She wanted to tell them she knew for sure that there was something else waiting for us after we died.

She wanted to have a grown up talk with them about Rachel, and to reassure them that Rachel was fine. But she couldn't. She had to keep all this information a secret, stored away with all her other secrets.

She was sure adults just wouldn't understand this stuff. Neither would other kids. The only person she could talk to about all these mysteries was Derek. And he would rather they didn't discuss them at all.

Madeline. Suddenly, that name popped into her mind.

Of course. Madeline understands this stuff. Derek and I have to go see Madeline, she thought, as sleep finally overtook her.

Derek sat in his room at his computer. The only light in the house was coming from the screen in front of him. He didn't feel sleepy, and he sat staring at old articles from 1882 that he found in the archives of the *Eastern Time News*. But this time, there was no tragic fire to report like the case of Isabel Roberts. He couldn't find anything about Abigail Baldwin. Maybe she just died from some kind of sickness, he thought. Or maybe it was just some simple farm accident that wasn't important enough to get into the paper. Or maybe her family wasn't prominent enough to bother writing about. The Roberts family had been well off, and active people in the community.

Ravine's sleep didn't stay peaceful for very long. As images arose inside her mind, she began to toss and turn. Eventually, she sat up and flicked on her bedside lamp. There was Abigail, still smiling. This time, though, Abigail was waving and reaching out for her. Ravine turned to look at her clock. Not quite three.

She got out of bed and staggered toward the mirror. As she reached out, a halo of light engulfed the mirror. Ravine could feel the soft touch of Abigail's hand, pulling her in. Once again, everything around her vanished into a pure whiteness, leaving her suspended in a world of nothing. But this time Ravine felt trapped, and her breathing became shallow. She grabbed at her throat and started to cough. She could still feel Abigail's hand on hers, but couldn't see her.

Suddenly, Ravine felt very dizzy. Just as she was about to pass out, Abigail suddenly jerked her into the past. As Ravine's breathing slowly returned to normal, Abigail's hand slipped away.

Ravine screamed for Abigail

Looking up, she saw Abigail's mother sitting

with Abe at the long wooden table. They were speaking in soft voices.

"Abigail!" Ravine called out. Abigail's parents ignored her.

"Ah, Meredith, you know how she gets. She'll be home any minute now," he said, reaching across the table to hold her hands.

"She has never been this late before, Abe. It's dark."

Her cheeks were wet with tears, and her eyes were swollen. She had been crying. This wasn't the first time Abigail was out late, or forgot about her curfew, Abe said. Abigail would forget her head if it wasn't attached.

"Meredith, she's out riding Gent. She handles that horse better than I can, and Gent would never let her fall. I know she's ridden off into the forest, but she knows those trees like the back of her hand. She just got distracted, like she did the other night. It's always darker in the forest, so sometimes you don't notice that it's getting late."

He wished Meredith wouldn't worry so much. But nothing was going to change her. He patted her hand and smiled.

"Why don't I saddle up Lady, and see if I can't find her."

"Oh, Abe, please. I am worried something

awful about that girl," she said, squeezing his hand tight.

Abe stood up, his chair scraping the floor. His big black boots thudded and echoed in the room as he headed for the door.

"Don't you worry, Meredith, I'll find Abigail."

Ravine followed him out the door, and across the yard to the barn.

"Lady, old girl, we're going for a ride tonight," he said, patting the old mare on her back. She whinnied, and nuzzled his chin. "You're going to get straw in my beard, my dear," he said.

He quickly saddled the horse and led her up the hill to the narrow gravel road.

"C'mon, Lady. We're going to find Gent and Abigail. And we're not coming back 'til we got 'em."

Ravine walked back out of the barn and into the warm summer night, just as Abe mounted the horse and headed off into the forest. It wasn't completely dark yet, but she could already see stars twinkling like diamonds in the clear sky. From experience, she knew Abe was right about how it was darker under the trees.

Looking through the window from the yard, Ravine could see Meredith sitting at the table with her head in her hands.

She couldn't go with Abe, and she wouldn't be able to follow without a horse of her own. She stood for a few minutes, staring off into the distance, wondering why Abigail was so late. When she no longer heard the echo of Lady's hooves, she walked back to the cabin.

Slowly, Ravine walked through the door as if it weren't there, and stood in the kitchen watching Meredith. Instinctively, she went over and touched the woman's shoulder.

Meredith whirled around. "Abigail!"

No one was there. She felt her shoulder where Ravine had touched it, and Ravine could see her trembling. Slowly, Meredith sat down again, cupping her head in her hands.

Ravine backed away. What was happening? Did she feel me touch her?

Climbing the ladder to the loft, Ravine stood in front of the mirror and looked around the room. She felt that something was very wrong, but she had no idea what. Anxious to go home, Ravine gazed at her reflection and then placed her hand on the cold glass. Nothing happened. Scared by the thought of being trapped in Abigail's world, she pushed harder. Finally, the mirror obeyed, and Ravine was gone.

Home at last, she crawled into bed and pulled the covers up to her chin. Ignoring the reflection in the mirror, she turned over and shut her eyes tight.

It was almost dawn. Derek had just switched off his computer, but he was still sitting at his desk, with his feet up. His desk lamp was on, and his sketchpad was on his knee. But there was not even a mark on the page, even though he had been twiddling the pencil in his fingers for about half an hour.

He tapped his knee with the pencil and swiveled back and forth in his chair, all the while softly humming under his breath. He couldn't quite remember the tune he was humming, but it sounded familiar to him.

With the next swivel of the chair, he caught a reflection in his dresser mirror and gasped. The pencil dropped from his hands and landed softly on the floor. His heart raced. A shadowy figured flickered in and out of focus, and Derek stood up. His legs felt like jelly. The bile in his stomach rose to his mouth, and he swallowed hard. He backed away, stumbling on the edge of the bed.

The figure in his mirror was grey, the colour of death, her hair wet with slime and her eyes wide but dead looking. Floating in a pool of water.

Derek wanted to scream, but as soon as he opened his mouth, the figure vanished, leaving him alone. He grabbed his sketchpad, and as quickly as he could, drew a picture of what he had just seen.

Chapter 8

Ravine woke Sunday morning to the sound of heavy rain beating against her window. She rolled over, and smiled at Abigail.

"Morning, Abby," she said softly. Abigail smiled as if she could hear her. Ravine lay in bed watching the girl in the mirror and as the sound of thunder echoed through her room, Abigail's reflection flickered.

"Are you always going to be in there? Or will you vanish too, once we find out what happened to you?"

Ravine lay with her head still in her pillows, and Abigail answered Ravine's questions with the same beautiful smile. Ravine didn't expect a reply. She already knew what was going to happen, and it made her sad. Just like Isabel, someday Abigail would be gone. Although she was worried, and didn't know what it was she was supposed to do, she thought it was important that Abigail not see her concern.

Ravine closed her eyes tightly and thought about Isabel. Immediately, Isabel appeared in her mind, holding out a bouquet of forget-me-nots.

"Never forget, my sweet Ravine," she whispered inside Ravine's head.

"Never forget, Isabel," Ravine whispered back.

Ravine climbed out of bed just as a streak of lightning flashed close to her window, followed within seconds by a huge crack of thunder. Even though it was morning, the sky was still dark. The clouds hung close to the ground, making it a terrible day to be outside.

As Ravine got dressed, she chatted away to Abigail. She jumped when the bedroom door suddenly opened.

"Who are you talking to?"

"Just myself, Mom" Ravine quickly answered.

"And are the two of you having an interesting conversation?"

Ravine blushed, but then added, "No. In fact we were arguing, and I keep losing. Mom, the other me is a lot smarter than the regular me."

Her mother looked at her and nodded.

"Well, breakfast is ready. I'm sure I made enough for both of you."

Ravine followed her mother downstairs to the smell of bacon and French toast. She realized she was very hungry.

"Good morning," her father said, cheerfully, as he was busy setting the table for three. "Did the storm wake you?"

Ravine shrugged. She was still pretty tired.

"Robbie, I think we need to set a fourth place. Ravine has been talking to herself, and I invited both of them to breakfast."

"Oh, Mom!"

Another sudden bolt of lightning shot through the sky, and the lights went out.

"Well, at least breakfast is cooked," her mother said, as her father went feeling through the dim light for some candles.

Her father lit five tall candles and set them in the middle of the table. The light from the flames cast shadows on the wall. Three shadows are what her parents could see; but Ravine saw four. She always knew that Rachel was nearby.

Her parents chattered on like it was just another ordinary Sunday breakfast. But as Ravine looked up, she sat frozen, staring at the shadow in front of her. She closed her eyes. This wasn't Rachel's shadow. This shadow was much taller than Rachel, and she knew instantly from the silhouette that she was looking at Abigail's outline.

The shadow didn't appear to be paying any attention to Ravine. It was looking off to the side, and obviously looking down at something. Ravine couldn't tell if the shadow was seated or standing, because the wainscoting in the kitchen distorted the lower part of the shadow.

Then, without any warning, it looked as if Abigail plunged off the side of something, or fell from where she was. It was too blurry to make out what was happening.

Ravine gave a small gasp, but her parents didn't notice because just at that moment, the lights flickered back on.

"Well, that wasn't very long," her mother said, blowing out the candles.

"So, Ravine," her father said, "are you still sure you aren't going out for trick or treat tonight? I ran into Sunil's dad the other day, and he was telling me you and Derek are the only ones in your crowd who aren't going out."

"I'm sure, Dad. Derek and I agreed we should let the small kids get all the candy. We'll both just stay home and help give it out."

She paused.

"But if there happens to be any left over …"

Derek grabbed his raincoat and slid his runners on his feet, trying to force them on without untying the laces.

"Where are you going?" his mom asked, watching him struggle with his shoe.

"Just over to Ravine's house," he answered. He reached for the door hoping his mom wouldn't stop him.

"Well, make sure you take an umbrella," she said.

He was thinking of saying umbrellas were for girls, but decided to let it go. He grabbed the umbrella and reached for the door handle.

"And Derek? The next time you're going out somewhere, you would be amazed how much easier it would be if you actually untied the laces before stuffing your feet into the shoes."

"Yes, Mom."

He headed out the door and raced down the steps.

The rain had already formed mini lakes on the sidewalk, and Derek splashed his way to Ravine's. By the time he got there, only two houses away, his pant legs were soaked and clinging to his legs like plastic wrap.

He stood on the verandah shaking himself like

a wet dog, then knocked loudly on the door as he listened to thunder rumble low in the sky.

Ravine's mother opened the door.

"Don't just stand there, Derek. Come in, come in!" She took his arm and shut the door quickly behind them. "Have you had breakfast?"

He nodded, and thanked her for the offer.

"Ravine's in her room," she said, as she took his wet umbrella. She put it on a boot mat to let it drip dry. "Are the lights back on at your place?" she asked, as she left him to go into the living room. He looked at her, not having any idea what she was talking about.

He nodded. "We have lights."

Derek climbed the stairs and walked into Ravine's room without even so much as a knock or hello.

She was sitting cross-legged on the floor in front of the mirror. Abigail was smiling in the mirror.

"Abigail was killed," Ravine said, still staring stone-faced at the mirror. Derek walked over to the bed and sat down beside her.

"I saw her falling. I don't know, it was all pretty strange, especially since I saw this on my kitchen wall. The weird thing was, no one could see this but me."

"I don't know what you're talking about," Derek said. "Slow down and start over."

"When the power went out, I saw her shadow on the wall, and then there was another shadow. But I don't know what that other shadow was. Oh, Derek it was terrible! I'm sure she was pushed." She was sobbing.

"When did the power go out?" he asked.

Ravine looked confused.

"This morning," she said. "Just as we were having breakfast. So about half an hour ago."

They stared at each other.

"The lights didn't go out this morning."

"They did here…"

They turned to look at Abigail in the mirror. But she just kept on smiling.

"Just because she fell, doesn't mean someone killed her," Derek said.

He handed Ravine the sketch he had drawn earlier.

"What's this?"

"I don't know," he said. "But it's what I saw in my own bedroom mirror late last night. I couldn't be sure who it was; it was too blurry. But I thought it looked like Abigail."

"People don't just fall for no reason, Derek. So somebody must have pushed her. But who?"

"Maybe it was an accident," Derek said. "People can fall off things. Do you remember David Brown who was in our grade one class? His father died when he fell off a ladder on a construction site. Nobody pushed him."

Abigail floated toward the mirror, reaching her hand out to them, coaxing them back into her world. But as Abigail motioned them toward her, Derek and Ravine reached for each other's hands and took a small step backwards.

Abigail's eyes widened, and Ravine felt as if she was being pulled into darkness. A darkness full of suffering.

Ravine unconsciously took a step closer to Abigail, but Derek yanked on her arm to hold her back. The pull from Abigail was stronger, and Ravine reached out to touch Abigail through the glass. Like a zap of electricity, she and Derek vanished once again, through the mirror.

Chapter 9

Abigail sat in a chair, watching as her mother rocked Abigail's new baby brother. The baby was swaddled in a cream blanket, and even though Abigail couldn't see him, she could hear his breathing and a soft bubbling noise.

"Shhhh. Now, now. Everything is okay."

Abigail's mother hummed in a singsong voice.

"Can I hold him, Mama?"

"When he's not fussing so much, dear." She went back to humming, with a dreamy look of contentment on her face.

Abigail crossed her legs and looked out the front window. Ever since the baby was born, her mother spent less and less time with her.

"Do you know how much I love you?"

Abigail looked up, but realized her mother was talking to the baby.

When Abigail was little, her mother used to sit on the bed with her and look out at the night stars.

"Do you know how much I love you, Abby?"

"No, how much do you love me?" Abigail would always ask her back.

Her mother would point to the brightest star in the sky and say, "All the way to that star and back again. That's how much I love you."

"Do you know how much I love you, mama?"

"How much do you love me, Abby?"

Then Abigail would jump into her lap and hug her tightly. "I love you that much, and lots more."

They'd sit on the bed and look into the sky, imagining how many stars there were.

"Which star is Papa?"

She asked the same question every night, and every night her mother would give the same answer, "The brightest star in the sky."

Abigail's father was killed when Abigail was just four years-old. She remembered that night, although she didn't understand it at the time.

Her father always worked long hours on Lawrence Matthew's farm. Each night, Abigail's mother had a hot meal waiting for him when he got home. Abigail would help her set the table, even though she could barely reach the top of it. But she could carry the knives and forks. They could always hear him riding up the gravel path, so they knew when he was coming. Just before he walked through the door, the food would be taken off the wooden stove. As the last dish was put on the table, her father's footsteps would echo on the stairs.

But that night had been a special night. It was her father's birthday, and her mother had made something he really liked. She had even saved up enough spare money to get the ingredients to bake him a pie.

But tonight, he was later than usual. Abigail fidgeted in her chair, and her mother stared at the door, as the time slowly ticked by. It was an hour later when loud footsteps were heard outside. Lawrence Matthews ran frantically up the steps, rushing inside without knocking.

Abigail still remembered the look of horror on her mother's face when Lawrence described the accident. Her father's horse had been spooked by the sound of a gunshot, and he had been thrown. He hit his head on a rock and was killed instantly.

Abigail cried that night because her mother was crying. She didn't understand what had happened, and she didn't realize she would never see her papa again. But she knew she couldn't give him a big birthday kiss.

Every night after that, her mother had told her that her father had traveled high up into heaven, and was now a bright star shining down on them. The brightest star in the sky, that was her papa.

"You can hold the baby now, Abigail." Abigail looked up. Her mother was standing in front of her with the sleeping baby.

"Come sit on the rocking chair, sweetheart. It's much more comfortable."

Abigail took a seat, and Meredith placed the tightly wrapped little bundle in her arms.

"Am I holding him right?"

"You are doing just fine. Little Fredrick is lucky to have such a wonderful sister."

Abigail was rocking back and forth, singing to the baby when the back door swung open.

"Hi, Abe," Abigail said sweetly. "Please don't let the door slam."

"Hey, Abigail, how's my girl?"

"Good, but you should lower your voice. The baby is sleeping," Abigail said softly.

Abe had been in Abigail's life for five years now. It wasn't easy for Abigail to let him in, especially since she thought of him as a replacement for her father. It took a couple of years for Abigail to be kind to Abe. She would call him names, sticking out her tongue at him behind his back, and crossing her arms over her chest shouting, 'I don't have to listen to you. You're not my real father!'

But eventually, he won her over. He never yelled at her, never hit her, and he even covered up for her when she forgot to do her chores. He was silent as a rock, waiting patiently to become a real father to her.

One night, when Abigail was searching out the brightest star from her bedroom window, she overheard a conversation between her mother and Abe. It was that night when she realized for the first time that Abe really loved her and her mama.

"She makes your life so miserable. I would understand if you want to leave," her mother said.

"No, Meredith. I married you because I love you. I knew it wasn't going to be easy, especially for Abigail. I can never be her real father, but I hope that she will accept me into her heart some day. I do love her, and everyday I love her more and more. She is a fine young girl, and she is our child, even if she doesn't see it that way. Yet. I'm not going to give up on her."

Abigail was surprised when the baby was named Fredrick. That was her real papa's name, and it was Abe's idea to name the baby after him.

"And take off your boots," said Abigail sternly. "They make too much noise on the floor. You could wake up little Fredrick."

Meredith smiled as she watched Abigail rocking her baby brother.

The door slammed as Henry entered and grunted his hello. The commotion finally woke the baby. His face turned red, he gulped a few times, and then let out an ear piercing scream. Abigail looked up and frowned.

"You can't come barging into this house like that, Henry Adams. Not anymore. There's a new baby here," said Abigail angrily. "Now you woke him, and it's going to take Mama all night to get him back to sleep."

Abigail stood up and handed Fredrick to her mother.

"Who made you the queen bee?"

Henry was thirteen, and he was an arrogant boy who didn't like to be bossed around.

"I did," said Abigail. "Do you have a problem with that?"

Henry stood in front of Abigail with his hands folded over her chest. He towered over her.

"Your bossy ways is going to get you into a lot of trouble some day," he snarled. He had the same thick curly hair as Abe. He stared at Abigail and his dark eyes bore into hers. But Abigail wasn't backing down. She wasn't afraid of him.

"That's enough, Henry," said Abe. "Sit down and get some grub. We still have to go back to the barn and finish loading the hay."

Abigail sat at the kitchen table across from Henry, watching him fill his bowl. He looked like a pig bellying up to the trough for his daily meal, she thought. She was disgusted watching him chew with his mouth open. Abigail could see the food slopping around in his mouth as he chomped it into smaller chunks. When he lifted his spoon to his mouth, soup ran down his chin.

Abigail tried to ignore Henry and eat her own meal. Then he let loose with a very loud belch.

"You are disgusting! You have the table manners of a pig."

Henry banged his spoon on the table and stood up, leaning toward her.

"And no one --"

"That's enough," said Abe. "If you're finished with dinner, let's go. There's a lot of work that needs to be done, and I don't want to be out all night."

Abigail started to apologize to Abe, but he stopped her.

"You're right. He does need some better manners."

Henry said nothing.

After Abe and Henry left, Abigail cleared the table and started to do the dishes. Meredith continued rocking Fredrick, who had actually managed to fall asleep again very quickly, despite what Abigail had said.

"Can I go out now, mama?"

"It's going to get dark soon, Abigail. Maybe some other night."

"Oh, please. I won't stay out late. And it's not dark yet. Please? Abe and Henry are out in the barn and I won't go out of the yard. How much trouble can I get into?"

"Okay, but make sure you stay in the yard. No heading into the forest when it's dark."

Abigail hugged her mother, then skipped out the door.

The sun was starting to set, and Abigail wandered aimlessly around the yard. Mama said she didn't want her out in the forest when it was dark. But it wasn't dark yet; the sun was only just beginning to set. She could hear Abe and Henry banging around inside the barn. Behind her the house was quiet.

The sun was finally setting when Meredith

stood on the back porch calling to Abigail. Abe and Henry appeared from the barn.

"Have you seen Abigail?"

"She came into the barn and asked to get Gent saddled," Henry replied, looking around. "She took him for a ride, but I ain't seen her come back."

"But its dark. She should be home by now," Meredith said. Fredrick could be heard inside as he started to wail, and Meredith rushed back inside to get him.

Chapter 10

Derek and Ravine walked to school Monday morning, chatting about last night's Halloween trick-or-treaters. They would have preferred to talk about Abigail, but they had barely left the house when Sunil wandered by and joined them. He was usually waiting at school when they arrived because his mother drove him on her way to work. But her car was in the shop getting fixed, so she was taking the bus today.

"Man, did I ever get a good haul," said Sunil. "I can't believe you guys didn't want to go out."

"We were feeling sorta Halloweened out, because of the dance," Derek answered. "Besides, it was nice to be able to see all the other kids' costumes without having to run from door to door."

"Some of the little kids were really cute," added Ravine. "There was this one kid, probably about five years-old. He was just dressed in regular clothes, except they looked like they were too big for him. So I asked who was supposed to be. He said he was pretending to be his big brother. Those were his brother's clothes, and so far nobody had figured that out."

As they reached the school yard, Sunil ran off to talk to Joannie. But after just a few steps, he turned and said, "Glad to see you guys are friends again."

It was the end of the school day before they had a chance to talk about Abigail. Sunil was staying late to play some basketball, and was a little disappointed that Derek didn't want to stay with him.

As they walked home, they talked about the scene they had witnessed yesterday when they were pulled into the mirror together. As far as they knew, Abigail didn't notice they were there watching the scene in the kitchen.

"That Henry gives me the creeps. There's something not right about him," Derek said.

"He seems to really hate Abigail, doesn't he?"

"And he seems so angry," Derek added.

The air was crisp. As they pushed through the cool wind, Ravine's eyes began to tear and her nose started to drip. She sniffed a couple of times, wiping her nose on her sleeve.

"It's only the first of November, but I bet it snows

before morning," Ravine blurted out. Her eyelashes felt frosty every time she blinked.

"It sure did get cold since yesterday."

After a few minutes of silence, Derek asked, "Why does Abigail only come to us through the mirror?"

Ravine knew Derek well enough to know he had been puzzling over that all night. She wondered how much sleep he got.

"What is it about this mirror? I don't get it."

"That's easy," Ravine replied. "I read about this stuff somewhere. It's a portal between her world and ours. I read that there are lots of them, but we just don't know where they are or how to go through them. The book said we usually only find them because somebody on the other side of the portal comes looking for us."

"That's weird."

They were entering Water Street now, and Lisa zoomed by on her bicycle. She looked frozen by the wind.

"I'm glad everything's back to normal with you guys," she said, as she zipped by.

"As normal as they ever will be," Ravine replied. She looked at Derek and smiled.

They were both very tired and went to bed early.

Neither of them was bothered by strange dreams during the night, and nobody awoke to find Abigail waving at them.

By lunch the next day, large snow flakes were drifting to the ground. Halloween was barely over, and winter looked to be coming fast. It was still a long way to Christmas, but the lunchroom was filled with excited chatter, as the kids watched everything slowly turn white. The white trees and white rooftops sparkled in the afternoon sun, bringing that magical feeling indoors.

Most important, it meant snowball fights on the way home.

Derek and Ravine sat alone at the lunchroom table, with their heads close together, as all their friends stood by the large window.

"How did you get back without going through the mirror?" Ravine ignored the excitement around her. "I always have to use the mirror to come back."

"I don't know," Derek replied in a whisper. "I fell off a cliff. And just when I thought I was going to hit the water, everything went black. Next thing I knew, I was back in your room. I thought I was going to die."

Ravine thought for a moment. "So we can travel through the mirror to go back in time, but from

Abigail's world, we don't need the mirror to come back. I wonder if that means we can get into her world without going through the mirror. Or maybe it just means that you can travel without the mirror, and I can't."

"I don't know," Derek began. "What if that was just a fluke? Or what if that portal, or whatever it's called, isn't open all the time? Have you been able to go through the mirror when Abigail isn't in it?"

Ravine thought about that, and shook her head. Derek had a point. Maybe it was too dangerous to travel back without using the mirror. They didn't even know where else they could find another portal.

"You're right," Ravine began. "Portals can't be open all the time, or people everywhere would just start disappearing with no explanation at all."

Derek agreed.

"Whoa!" he exclaimed.

"What?"

He didn't answer.

"Derek? What are you thinking?"

He started slowly. "Do you remember last summer when we were trying to find out if anybody besides us could see Isabel's house? Remember?"

Ravine nodded.

"Well," he continued, "we had always been

scared of number 56. But when it turned out none of our friends could see it, they started telling stories about it. Sunil told us about those construction workers that disappeared when they walked on to the empty lot at 56. No one could explain where they had gone."

Ravine was nodding her head faster now, and her eyes were getting big.

"Isabel created a portal," said Derek, "and I bet those workers were transported back into time, or somewhere else. It was the only way for Isabel to keep people away from there. After she did that, people stayed away. She closed the portal because no one was interested in that lot anymore."

"And when we came along," Ravine continued, "she didn't want to drive us away. She decided we could help. You're right. It frightened her to think that somebody would build on her property. If they had done that, she would have never been able to summon anyone to help her. And she would have never been able to go home. It all makes perfect sense."

"There you go again," Joannie exclaimed, as she sat down at the table. "Always whispering to each other."

"We're just talking about the history assignment that's due next week," Derek volunteered.

Joannie waved to Annie, and she came over to join them. Soon Lisa and Sunil were there as well, and the topic really did turn to the history assignment.

"So what are you guys doing for your papers?" Lisa asked

"King Tut," said Sunil immediately.

He shoved Derek over and plunked himself between Ravine and Derek. The group groaned.

"Well, why wouldn't I? I'm an expert. You all saw what a perfect King Tut I was at the Halloween party. I won the prize for best costume, didn't I?"

"You're obsessed, Sunil," said Ravine.

"What about you?" Sunil asked Lisa.

"Dracula."

"Dracula? That's just a movie monster," said Joannie.

"No, it isn't," said Derek. "The monster in the movies is based on a real guy. He really did live in a place called Transylvania, a few hundred years ago. Wow, I wish I had thought of him."

Just then the bell rang, and it was time to get back to class.

As they made their way back to class, Ravine and Derek walked a few steps behind everyone.

"Who are you doing your paper on?"

"Well, I thought about doing something on The

Roberts Family," said Derek. "But I figured you would probably do that."

Ravine laughed. She hadn't picked them either, thinking Derek would want to write about them.

"So then I thought of Shakespeare," he continued. "But I hadn't really made up my mind until just now when everybody said what they were doing. I'm gonna write about Chris Hadfield. You know, the Canadian astronaut who got to fly in space with NASA. He's from around here. And besides, I thought that might make me the only one to write about somebody who's still alive."

Ravine nodded.

"So are you writing about Isabel Roberts and her family?"

Ravine shook her head. "No, I assumed you were going to do that because you did all that research in the summer. To be honest, I don't know yet. I haven't started. I haven't even thought …"

Derek stopped in his tracks. Ravine was always miles ahead of everybody else with assignments. She wasn't just the smartest kid in class, she was also the best prepared.

"Don't look at me like that. I've been busy, you know." She smiled. "I'll figure something out," she said light-heartedly. "And it will be great."

Then they walked into the classroom together.

Mrs. MacDonald was waiting at the front of the classroom, looking very unhappy. Everybody quieted down and took their seats, wondering what was up. She was always so cheerful.

"Some of you," she started, "know there is a boy in one of the grade eight classes, who has gotten into trouble at school a few times."

Everyone knew exactly who she meant, and they all turned to look at Tyler. The boy was Ronnie Craigen, and most of the kids in Derek and Ravine's class thought he was a bully. But Tyler thought he was pretty cool, and often tried to hang around wherever Ronnie was.

"You may have seen him getting into fights in the schoolyard, or you certainly heard about it. Usually, he picks on smaller kids."

Mrs. MacDonald sounded angry now, but she quickly hid her feelings again, and continued.

"Twice in the past he has been suspended from school for fighting or being a bully. And he has been warned many times. This time, it has gone too far."

Everybody looked intently at the teacher. She had their full attention.

"On Friday night, Ronnie Craigen came to the Halloween party dressed like a gangster. The teachers on duty kept a close eye on him, especially when he started pushing his way around the gym. He bumped into one of the kids in his own class, and no one was sure if that was an accident. But then they started shoving each other, and just as Mr. Blackmore arrived to break it up, Ronnie pulled a big knife out of his jacket."

She paused to let that sink in.

"Ronnie Craigen's parents have transferred him to another school, and he won't be coming here any more. I'm not sure where they are going to send him, but he won't be here."

Lessons were shelved for the afternoon. Mrs. MacDonald led the class in a discussion about bullying, and what the kids should do if they saw, or were victims of, bullying. She was very passionate when she talked about the dangers of weapons. All the kids had things to say, even Tyler, who admitted that he had looked up to Ronnie. But he was sorry now, and he apologized to anyone who he might have upset by sticking up for Ronnie.

After school, Derek and Ravine decided not to go straight home. There was someone they needed to visit.

They walked for a while in silence, still thinking

about Ronnie Craigen and the discussion about bullies.

"I think Tyler was pretty brave today," Ravine finally said.

"Me too. But I'm glad Ronnie's gone. That guy was bad news."

They crossed the road and walked further along Quail Street, until they turned on to Swan Road. This was one of the oldest streets in town, dating back to the early 1800s when Summerhill was first settled.

Traffic on Swan was divided by a wide boulevard so full of large old trees that the cars going in one direction couldn't see the cars on the other side. Most of the houses lining the street had large trees on their lawns. The trees on the lawns and the boulevard overhung the road, and it was like driving through a tunnel. A car or even a van could drive along Swan without scraping its roof against tree branches, but a truck couldn't.

Because of the canopy created by the trees, it always seemed darker and cooler on Swan Road.

"I wonder which house Madame Jewels lives in," Derek said.

Last June, Derek and Ravine hired Madame Jewels to read fortunes at the end-of-school carnival. Madame Jewels, or Madeline in real life, had turned out to be something more, and something less, than they had expected. But she had understood the mystery of 56 Water Street, and had even been in the house herself. It was her who had put them on the right path to solving the mystery of the hundred-year-old ghost.

"Number 28."

"How do you know that?"

Ravine shrugged.

"I don't know. The number just popped into my head when you asked."

She pointed across the street to a red brick house with a Japanese maple. The snow that had fallen earlier had melted in most places, but in the shadows of Swan Road, it remained. The maple had not yet lost its leaves, and the snow clinging to the branches made it look beautiful.

"Are you sure?" Derek asked. He didn't like the idea of knocking on some stranger's door.

"Absolutely."

They crossed the street and climbed the concrete steps. Just as Ravine was about to ring the bell, Madeline opened the door, smiling.

"Hi, Derek. Hi, Ravine. I knew you were coming, so I thought I'd save you the trouble of ringing the bell. Come in," she said.

Madeline guided Derek and Ravine through a big oak door into a foyer painted gold and white.

Odd choice of colour, Derek thought.

"How did you know we were coming?"

Derek liked Madeline, but her ability to see things that other people couldn't frightened him. It didn't seem to occur to him that, well, so could he.

"She's a psychic. Of course she knew we were coming," Ravine said.

Madeline laughed. "No, I just saw you crossing the street."

She led them into a large square living room. The entrance to each of the rooms leading off the foyer was framed by ornate white pillars. The walls in the living room were painted the same gold as the foyer. All the living room furniture was white.

"Man, you must really like gold and white," said Derek, looking up at the high ceilings. There was a swirled pattern in the ceiling plaster, along with crown moldings trimmed in white and gold. The floor was white ceramic tile.

"I do. They are the main colours of my aura, so I like to surround myself with those colours. They are pleasing to my eye, and to my mind."

Derek nodded, even though he had no idea what she was talking about.

"What's an aura?" asked Ravine.

Derek groaned. He wasn't too sure he wanted to know.

"Your aura is the energy that surrounds your body. Everyone has one, but not everyone can see it. Most people can't see someone else's aura. The energy is made up of different colours, for different people. Mine is gold and white."

"Do the colours mean something?" Ravine asked.

Derek watched Ravine. She always lit up when she was with Madeline. He knew Ravine felt a very strong connection to this woman. Madeline was the first person Ravine had opened up to about Rachel's death. In fact, Derek had not even heard her say Rachel's name, until she talked to Madeline.

"Gold and white are signs of high spiritual development, joy, and happiness. Being able to see the big spiritual picture. But our auras change from time to time. Kind of like our moods."

Madeline motioned them to sit on the white sofa. As Derek and Ravine sank into the cushions, Madeline brought out a bowl of nuts and a pitcher of orange juice. Derek and Ravine glanced at each other, but said nothing about the strange snack.

Madeline was an ordinary looking woman. Her blonde hair fell in shoulder length curls, her big round eyes were a brilliant blue, and her lips were pencil thin.

But it was only her appearance that was ordinary.

Madeline Jewels worked with the police force. She wasn't a police officer, but she used her psychic powers to help the police solve crimes when regular detective work failed. She was particularly successful with cold crimes and missing children cases.

"What brings you by?" she asked, sipping on her juice. She sat in the chair across from Derek and Ravine, with her legs curled under her.

Ravine explained to Madeline about the mirror and Abigail Baldwin. She tried to include everything she could remember. Then Derek added what he knew, telling the story of falling off the cliff and ending up back in Ravine's room. As they spoke, Madeline became very still and silent. Her breathing slowed as she listened intently.

When they had told her everything, Madeline shook her head.

"If anyone else was telling me they had travelled through time, I don't think I would believe them. But I do believe you. This is really quite extraordinary."

Madeline hesitated. "But I must warn you this

is very dangerous. I don't think you should do it again."

"But we have to," cried Ravine. "We need to help Abigail."

"Is there no way of helping her without going through the mirror?" Madeline asked.

"I don't think so," Derek replied.

They all fell silent.

Finally, Madeline spoke.

"What I'm going to tell you might sound strange. I guess most people wouldn't even understand it. But you've both gone through a portal and travelled to the past. Please, don't interrupt," she said, as Derek opened his mouth to say something.

"First, you need to know that the universe is a lot more complicated than we think. Scientists are concerned about the stars and galaxies. But some people believe there are different dimensions in the universe, sort of like parallel universes that all share the same space as the one we can see.

"And there are doors that separate the different dimensions. The doors are called portals, and they are highly unstable. When the doors are opened too frequently, they eventually break down and collapse, becoming completely unusable. These portals are not meant to be used by living people.

"It is quite surprising to me that you have been

able to pass through the portal of the mirror. And you, Derek, appear to have gone through a separate portal when you fell from the cliff."

Madeline paused.

"Frankly," she started again, "it is much too dangerous to keep going in and out of a portal like this."

"What's so dangerous about it?" Ravine asked.

"Like I said, when the doors are used too frequently by humans, they will eventually break down. Which means, some day they won't open anymore. Which also means you might not be able to get into her world, or worse. You might get in and not be able to get back out. You would be stuck in that other dimension forever."

Derek stared at his lap. "I just knew that mirror was bad. I just knew it," he muttered.

"But if the portals aren't for us to use, what are they for?"

Derek didn't care who or what they were for. All he cared about was that Madeline told them not to go through the mirror anymore. That was all he needed to hear. Madeline's word was good enough for him.

"They are for our angels," Madeline replied.

Derek snorted at that, but Madeline and Ravine ignored him.

"What angels?" asked Ravine.

Derek put his head in his hands. It was bad enough that he could see things other kids couldn't see. It was bad enough that he could talk to ghosts. It was way too much that he could travel back in time. Now there's angels?

"We all have angels," Madeline began. "They guide us through life. We each have our own angel, one who is with us from the time we are born, to the time we die. Our angels can take on many forms. They aren't like you see them in pictures, beautiful humans with wings. They can be any kind of animal, from cats to rats, or birds. Even lizards. And some of them do take the form of humans.

"There are other angels who come and go throughout different periods of our lives. They arrive when we need them, and leave when their work is done. The portals are for the angels, to come and go as needed. They created most of the portals themselves, so they could access the different dimensions and times."

Madeline paused to let this sink in.

"You see, we are not the only ones here," she continued. "In this place, there is more than just the universe we know. In fact, there are many universes, all taking up the same space, but in different dimensions. We just don't have the ability to see them."

Madeline paused again. She knew this was a difficult concept, and she could see Derek and Ravine were looking puzzled. She thought back to when someone had first explained all of this to her. It seemed like a lifetime ago.

Madeline continued. "I know it might not seem like it to you, but you haven't really gone back in time. Time is a concept created by humans, because we have a need to see things happening in some kind of sequence. And we need to think that everything must have a beginning and an end. We break down the interval between things into some kind of segments that we can measure, that we can count.

"There really is no such thing as time. So when you go through the portal in Abigail's world, you are not really travelling in time. You are really moving into her dimension, not her time."

Derek and Ravine sat quietly, staring at Madeline. They both understood what they had just heard, but it seemed unbelievable. If anyone other than Madeline had told them all of this, they would never accept a bit of it. But they knew Madeline, and they knew she was serious.

"We don't need to know all of this. We really don't," Derek blurted out.

Madeline smiled.

"Derek, I'm afraid you do need to know these things. You can try to ignore who you are, to deny that you have insights that other kids don't. But eventually, you are going to have to accept yourself for who you are. You can't run away from yourself."

"Are there bad angels?" Ravine asked.

Derek didn't hear Ravine's question. He was lost in his own thoughts, trying to digest everything he had just heard. How did all of that fit with his experiences? If he understood this correctly, when he and Ravine had visited with Isabel and Sarah as they were before they died, they weren't really back in time, but in another dimension.

The idea of other dimensions did not seem strange to him. But time was something else. He read lots of science, and he knew that time controlled everything. Einstein said that it was a dimension, like length and width. The clocks ticked, everything followed everything else, one thing at a time, in a logical pattern. Without time, life would be chaos. Everything might happen all at once.

"There are angels known as fallen angels," said Madeline. "But I wouldn't call them bad. It's more like they are misplaced. They haven't quite learned the concept of right and wrong. They are, I guess you would say, stuck in limbo, between dimensions. But those angels would never be able to cross through the portals."

"But why?" Ravine asked.

"Because they haven't been given the ability or knowledge. And until they learn the concept of right and wrong, they are stuck in between worlds. That is another reason why going through the mirror is so dangerous. The space inside the portals is where the fallen angels reside, and no one knows for sure how troublesome or hurtful they can be. Maybe one of them could capture you when you were passing through. I don't have any idea what would happen to you then."

"Do you think one of those bad angels could hang on to Derek or me and get through the portal that way?"

"No. They cannot. Their spirit body, or soul, or whatever you want to call it, is too transparent to let that happen. And because they aren't really alive either, they can't use the mirror the way you can. It's all very complicated, really, but I think there would be a bigger problem with one not letting you through at all. If you were trying to get into Abigail's world and couldn't get through, there would be no real harm. But if you did get through, one might be able to block you from getting back. That, along with the damage being caused to the portal with you going in and out, is what makes this so dangerous."

Derek wasn't listening to Madeline. His mind had drifted off, and he was thinking about all those people he couldn't see. What kind of people were they? The hair on his arms stood on end, and he jumped. He was sure someone invisible bumped into him.

Madeline laughed as she watched him.

"Our worlds don't collide that easily, Derek. Anyway, I know this is all very hard to understand. Frankly, even I have a difficult time understanding the whole concept. But the one thing you must understand, is that what you two are doing is very dangerous."

Derek looked at Ravine. Her eyes were twinkling.

"You said the angels created most of the portals. Who creates the other ones?"

"It doesn't matter, Ravine," said Derek. "The only thing that matters is that we should not be going through the mirror again."

But Ravine wasn't paying any attention to him. Her eyes were focused only on Madeline.

"Portals can be created by ghosts, like Isabel, who haven't crossed over yet, or by spirits that are troubled by their past and need answers. But those portals are just as unstable.

"Because the portals were never designed for humans, when we pass through them our bodies start to make them break down. The oils on our skin rub against the invisible barriers, creating an oily film between both worlds. Eventually this film becomes so thick that crossing through the portal becomes impossible. Not just for you, but for the angels too. That's why it is so important that you don't go through the mirror again. Especially since you have been through so many times."

Derek and Ravine sat silent. Ravine knew she needed to go through the mirror again, and Derek knew he was going to have to stop her.

"You have to promise me you will find another way to help Abigail," Madeline said sternly. "Knowing that you have been travelling through the dimensions really scares me. I don't want to go to work one day and find there is a missing children's case involving one or both of you."

"You don't have to worry, Madeline. Derek and I won't go through the mirror again. I am sure there must be another way of helping Abigail," Ravine said sweetly. "We'll find that way."

Derek was stunned. He knew that wasn't true. He couldn't remember Ravine ever telling a real lie, and he was horrified that her first one was to Madeline.

As they walked down Madeline's front steps, they turned to wave goodbye. She smiled at them and watched as they disappeared around the corner.

Derek and Ravine walked most of the way home in silence. As they reached Water Street, Derek was the first to speak.

"Now what?" he asked.

"Well," Ravine began slowly, "I guess we go back to the mirror."

"But didn't you hear what Madeline said," Derek exclaimed. He turned to Ravine and scowled. "Are you nuts? If Madeline is right, and we both know she is, it is way too dangerous to be messing with that mirror anymore. And you promised her you wouldn't go back through!"

"I had my fingers crossed behind my back."

"You lied!"

"I did," Ravine said. "But going through the mirror is the only way to find out what happened to Abigail."

Ravine ran up the driveway, opened the front door, and let it slam behind her.

"I'm home!" she yelled, throwing her jacket on the floor. She could smell supper, and headed to the kitchen, suddenly feeling very hungry.

Her parents were already eating.

"You're late," her mother said, without even saying hello. "I called Derek's house. His mother just assumed Derek was over here. We had no idea where the two of you were."

Ravine pulled up a chair.

"I am sooo sorry," she said. "We went to the library because we've got these history assignments coming up. I guess we lost track of the time. We ran home as fast as we could when we realized how late it was."

She reached for the tray of lasagna. "This smells good, Mom. Did you make it yourself?"

Her mother tried to hide her smile. "Next time, don't be so late. Keep an eye on the clock."

Derek slammed the door behind him and looked into the living room. He could hear his mother and Danielle fighting in the kitchen. Perfect timing, he thought. All he had to do was head upstairs and wait until someone called him down to supper. He took the stairs two at a time, and hid himself in his room, waiting for the battle to end.

He plopped himself on the bed and grabbed his basketball, throwing it up at the ceiling. There was homework to do, but his mind was still reeling with everything Madeline had told them this afternoon. And he was still shocked by Ravine's lie. More than anything else he had heard today, that was huge. He was disappointed, and the more he thought about it, the angrier at Ravine he became.

Finally, there was a knock on his door.

"Derek," his mother called, "It's time for supper."

As he heard her steps heading back down the stairs, she added, "And don't think you aren't going to answer for being so late, mister."

Ravine closed her bedroom door and sat in front of the mirror. She thought about everything that Madeline had told them this afternoon. She knew she shouldn't ignore what Madeline said, but she was convinced that going back through the mirror was the only way to help Abigail.

But help Abigail with what? It couldn't be to prevent her from being killed, because the gravestone at Summerhill Cemetery made it clear that she did die.

She decided to ignore the fact that she didn't even know what it was that Abigail needed help with.

Ravine already knew she had an angel, although she had never called it that. It wasn't what most people thought of when they heard the word angel. Her angel was a white tiger, and his name was Alexios. As far as she knew, he had been there all her life, although it was only a few years ago that she saw him for the first time. She would talk to Alexios sometimes when she was alone, although he never answered. At night, she often thought just as she was drifting off to sleep, that she could hear him purring softly at the foot of her bed.

There still were many things she knew, things she could see, that she hadn't told Derek about. Not yet. She knew he was still very uncomfortable with the abilities they shared, and she sensed he would have to learn these things a bit at a time.

She thought about Rachel, because it was her younger sister who had told Ravine about her angel.

"You have a pretty kitty," four-year-old Rachel had told her. They were both lying in bed staring up at the ceiling. The room was dark, lit only by the occasional brightness of headlights from passing cars.

"I don't know what you are talking about. I don't have a kitty. I would like to have one, but you know Daddy is allergic to cats," Ravine said.

She turned over to look at the outline of her sister. A night table separated the two single beds.

"He's with you all the time. He looks as soft as cotton, and he has dark chocolate stripes against his white fur. He's so pretty Ravine. And really big."

"Don't be ridiculous, Rachel. You're not making any sense. Your imagination is running wild."

Then there was silence. But Ravine couldn't shake Rachel's words. She was always talking like this, and every time she did, the hairs on Ravine's arms stood on end.

"So if I have a kitty, what do you have?" Ravine challenged.

"It's some kinda bird, but I don't know what kind. She has a really, pretty white head and she is really, really big. And she has a big yellow beak. Her feathers look so soft, but they aren't white like her head. They're brown. She has big claws and little yellow eyes, too."

It always made Ravine feel nervous when her sister talked like this, but she sounded so confident. It was almost like this bird and cat were sitting right in front of them.

"It sounds like an eagle. Does she have a name?"

"Uh huh. It's Aquila."

Ravine thought for a moment and then said. "How come I can't see them if they are real?"

"Because you don't believe they're here. Once you believe in them, you will see them. Aquila talks too. But not very often. For such a big bird, she has a very soft voice. I've never heard your kitty talking. It's funny how your cat and my bird get along so well."

"Yeah, that's really funny Rachel."

"Aquila told me that I am going to get sick and die, but I shouldn't be afraid of it. She said she will be with me always."

"Don't say things like that, Rachel. You are perfectly healthy." Ravine hated when Rachel spoke of death.

The room was silent and Ravine was deep in thought. She was about to ask Rachel if she knew the name of Ravine's big cat, but she heard her sister breathing heavily. Rachel had fallen asleep.

It was when Rachel finally became sick that Ravine first saw Alexios, her angel. Her white tiger. She remembered standing beside Rachel's bed holding her hand. She looked up and standing by the door was an enormous white tiger. She couldn't move.

"You see him, don't you?" Rachel asked in a tiny voice. "I told you so!"

From that day forward, Alexios had never left Ravine's side. She remembered endlessly talking to him at night when she was alone in her room. The room had become very empty with Rachel in the hospital. She had even caught herself a few times talking to him when her parents were around. After a strange look from her mother, it didn't take Ravine long to figure out she needed to be more careful.

And Ravine remembered the first time Rachel had told her about Aquila. The bird had predicted that Rachel was going to get sick, but it also said she was going to die. So all through Rachel's illness, when her parents were trying to keep hope alive, Ravine already knew that she would soon be saying goodbye to her sister for the last time.

After Rachel died, Ravine would find herself forgetting that Alexios was there. Sometimes she went days without even speaking to him. But that was okay, she figured. Most humans couldn't even see their angels. They were only there to protect, and to try to help people to make wise choices. But even so, Alexios always slept at the end of her bed and was never far from her.

Ravine came back to reality. She glanced over to her desk and glumly stared at a big stack of books. A book about Anastasia Romanov lay open, showing a picture of her and her brother Alexei. It was the story of the Russian Princess who was murdered along with her family. The story of Tsar Nicholas, the last Russian Tsar, had intrigued Ravine since she was small. The Romanov family had disappeared during the Russian Revolution, and for many years there had been rumours that Anastasia had escaped.

She was going to write her history assignment about Anastasia.

But not tonight.

Ravine took a step toward the mirror, and stretched her hand toward Abigail. Her history paper would just have to wait. She heard a growl from her bed, but she ignored it.

Without a second thought, she was sucked into the mirror.

Ravine found herself standing off to the side, arriving just in time to witness a fight between Abigail and Henry.

"You are the bossiest girl I ever know'd," Henry yelled.

"Well," Abigail said, "I suppose you haven't known very many girls." Her voice carried a tone of superiority.

"If you weren't a girl, I'd hit ya."

Ravine backed into the corner of the living room.

"And I'd make ya sorry for all the nasty things you say to me," he continued.

Abigail walked toward him and stood in front of him. Then, without any warning, she stomped hard on his foot.

"Why you little ..."

But before Henry could finish, Abigail was out the door and down the steps. Henry was right behind her, with Ravine following.

"If you ain't scared of me, what are you running away from?" he yelled after her.

Abigail stopped and turned to face him.

"Who says I'm afraid? I'm not afraid of you! Not even a mouse would be afraid of you."

"Well, you should be, Abby Baldwin. You should be afraid of me."

Chapter 11

The week went by quickly. It remained cold, and there was a little more fresh snow every day, that glistened like diamonds when the sun shone. The clear sky was the colour of a light blue crayon, and the sun shone low on the horizon like a little yellow ball. The sun was warm enough to feel on your face when the wind slowed, but the air was too cold for the snow to melt.

Ravine liked snow. But except for the white blanket and the sights of stores that were hanging early Christmas decorations, she had a terrible week.

At school that morning, she watched Derek as he took out his history assignment from his binder.

"Where's your paper?" he asked, leaning back on his chair.

Ravine shook her head, her face hot from

embarrassment. "I didn't get around to doing it," she said.

Derek gaped at her, just as Mrs. MacDonald, collecting everyone's papers, arrived beside Ravine's desk.

"Your assignment?"

Ravine turned her guilty-looking face to the teacher. She had no excuse for the assignment not being done, so she didn't even try. But she pleaded with Mrs. MacDonald to give her a couple more days.

"We'll speak about this later," the teacher said. She continued to collect everyone else's project.

When class was done for the day, Mrs. MacDonald called Ravine to her desk.

"I will give you two days to complete this assignment, Ravine. But only because this is so out of character for you. You have until Friday. Make sure your assignment is finished."

Ravine heaved a sigh of relief.

But then Mrs. MacDonald added, "However, I will have to phone your parents to let them know about this."

By the time she got home from school, she didn't even have to ask. She was sure her mother was going to ground her. And she was right.

After the lecture, Ravine slipped up to her room

and sat down in front of the mirror. A few minutes later, her mother knocked on the door. Instead of seeing Ravine sitting at her desk working on the history paper, she found her sitting on the floor staring at her reflection in the mirror.

"I don't know what it is with you and this mirror," her mother said. "But it's gone until you get that paper done."

She picked up the mirror, trying not to let on that it was so heavy. How on earth did this kid manage to carry this thing home from the shop, she wondered.

After her mother left, Ravine called Derek.

"Well," he said coolly, "she did say you could have the mirror back when you finish your paper. So, finish your paper."

"But you don't understand," she said, pacing her room with the phone. "I haven't even started it yet! I have to complete a three-week assignment in two days so Mrs. MacDonald will give me a good grade. And if I want to get the mirror back. If we don't have the mirror, we can't find out what happened to Abigail."

There was silence on the other end. Finally Derek said, "Well, I guess I better let you go. It sounds like you have a lot of work ahead of you."

He hung up.

Ravine slammed the receiver down, and stomped back and forth in her room. A tear escaped and ran down her cheek. She couldn't tell if she was angrier about the situation, or about the way Derek brushed her off. She stared at the empty spot where the mirror used to be, and suddenly felt hollow inside.

She took a deep breath and sat down at her desk. Opening a book entitled *The Murder of Tsar Nicholas and His Family*, she started to read.

Derek hung up the receiver, smiling, almost chuckling. Ravine was his best friend. He could never hope to find a better friend. But every once in a while, it was nice to see that people you look up to are not perfect. And he did look up to her. He admitted that to himself, although he had never told her. She'd just tell him to shut up and stop being a jerk.

Derek knew Ravine would finish her history paper on time, even if she had to go the next two nights without any sleep.

Laying down on his bed, he began to think about Henry and Abigail. With all that had gone on since they saw Madeline, he had forgotten to tell Ravine about his theory. He was positive Henry had something to do with Abigail's death. He didn't know how, or what Henry might have done, but he thought he could sense something evil in Henry. He grabbed the phone and started to dial Ravine's number, then quickly hung up. Better not, he thought. She has a lot of work to do, and this can wait. In fact, he decided he had better wait until she finished her paper so she didn't get distracted.

Lost in his thoughts, he jumped at the sound of a knock on his door.

His mother opened the door, and stood in the entrance with a serious look on her face.

"I have something for you," she said.

She held out a white envelope and handed it to Derek. Derek read the name of the sender and frowned.

"Why are you giving this to me?" His forehead creased and his smile disappeared.

"Because it's addressed to you."

Derek shook his head. "I don't want it."

He tried to hand it back to his mother but she had her arms crossed.

"It's up to you whether you read it or not. I'm not going to force you to read something you don't want to, and I'm not going to tell you what I think you should do. But it's yours, and you should have it. You'll have to make up your own mind what to do with it."

she kissed him on the forehead.

"Derek, I will always love you. No matter what you do."

Then she shut the door behind her.

Derek threw the envelop on his desk and walked out of his room wondering if this had anything to do with all those weird phone calls.

Ravine finished her history paper on time, and after class on Friday, she sat at her desk as Mrs. MacDonald read it over. Occasionally, the teacher glanced up at Ravine and then went back to reading. Finally, she took out her big red marker and graded the paper.

"Here you go," she said. Ravine walked to the front of the class and Mrs. MacDonald handed her paper back.

"From anyone else, this is a fine paper. But from you, this is a little disappointing. Your work is usually much better," she said in a soft voice.

Ravine looked at her grade. It was a B minus.

"I hope whatever problem has gotten you so distracted, you find a solution to it soon. I would hate to see your grades suffer. I've looked back at your marks from other years. No teacher has ever given you any grade except an A. Neither have I, and I hope I never have to do it again."

Derek was waiting for Ravine in the hall, leaning against the wall with his backpack slung over his shoulder.

"Well? How did it go?"

Ravine felt butterflies well up in her stomach. But as quickly as they came, they left.

"Not well," she replied. "I got a B minus."

"Wow! I bet you won't do that again."

As Derek opened the door, a cold wind swept past their faces. It was still early in November, but already it was feeling like winter. Derek buried his chin deep into his jacket. Ravine left her jacket unzipped.

"You sound like my mother," she finally said.

They quickly walked out of the school ground, pushing against the strong wind.

"Well, in that case," he said, "you better do up your jacket. You'll catch your death of a cold if you don't."

Ravine looked up at him, but before she could reply, he smiled and winked.

It was Saturday night before Ravine saw her mirror again. But before that, came a long lecture about school work, home work, and how the decisions Ravine made today would affect her in the future. She nodded her head throughout the hour-long lecture.

Ravine agreed with every comment, and she assured her parents this would never happen again.

Finally, Ravine closed the bedroom door behind her and walked over to the mirror. She looked at her own reflection, and the reflection of the blonde haired girl. Her smile was as sweet as honey.

Ravine picked up the phone and dialed Derek's number.

"Come over," she said. "Abigail's back."

Derek and Ravine held hands in front of the mirror.

"I don't know about this," Derek said, remembering Madeline's words.

"It's the only way to save her," Ravine replied.

Chapter 12

Abigail led her mother outside into the fresh warm summer breeze. It had been two weeks since the baby's birth. Abigail spread a blanket on the ground and sat down with her mother.

"Can I hold him?"

Her mother nodded, placing the baby gently on Abigail's lap.

Abigail and her mother sat in the middle of a flower patch, looking like two young girls. Despite the trials of her life, Meredith looked as if she could be the older sister.

They watched Abe and Henry working to fill in the old well, pulling heavy decaying brick tiles from around the edge. Henry wiped his brow, looking down the dark hole.

"It's going to take all day to fill it in," Henry said.

"Oh, I think it's going to take at least a few

days," Abe exclaimed, taking a breather too. "Bad luck for me that you weren't around when I had to dig the new well. That was a lot of work. I needed to dig closer to the stream, and pump it out from that direction over there. It's hard enough pumping water up hill, but you gotta wonder what old George Green was thinking when he dug the well so far from the creek."

Abe probably wouldn't have gone to all this work unless the well had run dry. But the bricks lining the original well were starting to decay and the walls were in danger of collapsing. He figured digging a new one was probably less work than fixing the old one, and he'd finally have a well further down the slope, closer to the water.

It was a big job, and even though he had to do most of it by himself, he was grateful for the help that Henry could give. Henry was a strong boy, and a good boy. But he was rough, and definitely needed to learn some better manners.

Henry nodded as his uncle spoke.

"Isn't it sorta dangerous having a hole this deep in the middle of the yard?" Henry asked. "The old well's been covered up for these past weeks now. But it's easy enough for the boards to get blown off, or knocked out of place. Then someone could fall in."

Abe agreed. But he said the boards would have to do until they could get the hole filled.

"I'll put some of the old bricks on top of the boards to make sure they stay put. But you and Abigail make sure to stay away from it until it gets filled in proper."

Abe turned around and watched Meredith and Abigail sitting in the middle of the wild daisies. Meredith looked so young, sitting with her skirt spread out on the grass. It was hard to believe just two weeks ago she gave birth to Fredrick. And watching Abigail sit with her brother on her lap, he smiled. The girl had finally learned to like Abe, and now she was growing up so fast.

Since Fredrick arrived, Abigail had taken on a lot of responsibility. She cared for the baby, and took over many of the chores from her mother. She swept the floors, kneaded the dough, and hung the laundry. And neither he nor Meredith had to remind her of her own chores any more. What a difference Fredrick had made in her life, he thought.

Meredith turned her gaze toward Abe and caught him looking at her. She smiled. He waved at her, and then went back to work.

"Well, let's do some more shoveling," he said to Henry.

When Henry didn't respond, Abe looked at him and found him staring at Abigail.

The men worked at filling the old well until the sun was high in the sky. It was strenuous work, and the scorching heat made it seem much harder. Henry turned toward Abigail and Meredith, just as they were getting up and folding their blanket.

"We're going in to finish making lunch," Meredith called to them. "I'll send Abigail out when it's ready."

Abe watched as they headed toward the house. He knew that Meredith had been simmering a stew on the wood stove since early morning.

But Henry was busy watching Abigail. She had the same beautiful champagne hair as her mother, and it hung past her shoulders, down to the small of her back. Henry had never seen the ocean, but he'd heard songs that always said it was blue. He bet it wasn't anywhere near as blue as Abby's eyes.

"Let's keep going until lunch," Abe said. He nudged Henry in the shoulder. "The more we do now, the less we gotta do later."

Abe wiped his brow again, and they both got back at it. Abe pulled his shirt over his head and sweat trickled down his chest and back. His muscles were large from a lifetime spent working the land.

Henry followed, and pulled off his shirt. A white cotton undershirt clung to his drenched skin. His arms were bronzed from many long days in the sun and his muscles were beginning to develop. Although he was a strong lad, it would take many more years of hard work before he would be as big and powerful as his uncle.

It wasn't long before the door to the house opened and Abigail came skipping toward them.

"Lunch is ready," she said.

Abigail came closer and peered down the dark hole. Abe patted Abigail on the shoulder, telling her to be careful, as he turned to head toward the house.

Henry took a step closer toward Abigail. He was standing so close that she could feel the heat from his body. He looked down the hole.

"Don't play anywhere's near that hole, Abby," he said. "It's dangerous."

The look in his eyes told her he was serious.

"I think I'm a little too old for playing. But I will stay away from it," Abigail said, as Henry headed toward the house. But she stepped closer to the hole all the same, wanting to see how far down it went.

Henry quickly turned and came back to grab her by the shoulders. Abigail stumbled into him as he caught her and pulled her away from the hole.

"I told you to stay away from here. It's dangerous. I weren't fooling."

His eyes blazed, and she glared at him momentarily, trembling, before backing away from the well. She turned and ran to the house without another word.

That night, Abigail tossed and turned. Her dreams were fragmented and disturbing. In them, she saw visions of her father's smiling face. Around the outline of his body was a white glow, which made Abigail feel safe and happy. But then everything turned dark and she was staring into the angry face of Henry. She tried to run from him, but he chased her until she was standing at the edge of the old well.

"You don't want to get too close to the well," he laughed, coming toward her. "It's dangerous, Abby Baldwin. It's very dangerous. Don't get too close to the well, Abby," he said again, laughing. His eyes were blazing.

Then with a sudden push, Abigail could feel herself fall, and the echo of Henry's voice filled her head, 'it's dangerous, it's dangerous, it's dangerous.'

Abigail awoke with a jolt. Her nightgown was clinging to her body, and beads of cold sweat dripped down her face. Even though it was a warm summer night, she suddenly felt cold and pulled the covers up to her chin. She listened to the sound of silence all around her.

She was not a foolish girl, and she knew a hole in the ground by itself was not dangerous. As long as you knew it was there, you could be careful not to fall into it. No, it wasn't the hole she needed to stay away from. It was Henry.

Abigail awoke early the next morning, but she stayed in bed for a little while listening to rain on the roof and the comforting voices of her mother and Abe.

"Please don't delay, Abe. I looked at it when I went out to gather the eggs this morning. That hole looks real dangerous to me. One slip and ... well, I just hate to think about it."

"Aw, Meredith. Henry and me are working as hard as we can. Abigail knows to stay away from the hole. She's a smart girl. And we keep it covered if we have to go off and do some other chore. Besides, she spends so much time helping you with Fredrick, when would she ever go near it? If she had some time to herself, you know she'd be running off into the forest. That's where she's really happy."

Abigail smiled. She knew Abe was right.

"Besides," added Abe, "there ain't nothing more we can do about it today with all this rain."

Chapter 13

Later that week, Ravine lay in bed restless. She was fighting sleep because of a panicked feeling that if she closed her eyes, she would never wake up. She told herself over and again that this was ridiculous. But even so, each time her eyes became heavy and started to close, she would quickly open them again and try to think of anything that might keep her awake.

Gradually, she lost the battle and tumbled into a deep sleep.

All around her was darkness; but, oddly, she felt safe. As she breathed, a sweet scent of flowers drifted passed her. She could tell she was seated on soft ground, but she still had no idea where she was.

When she opened her eyes, she found herself sitting in the middle of forget-me-nots with Isabel.

"Never forget," Isabel said, smiling and handing Ravine a blue flower.

"Never forget," said Ravine.

They sat together beneath a clear blue sky, and no other words were spoken for a while. The colours in this dream seemed much more vibrant than in the real world, and Ravine was fascinated by the intensity of the light and the bright hues.

She finally looked toward the other girl and found Isabel smiling at her.

"Can I change fate?" Ravine searched deep into Isabel's eyes. "I mean, is it possible to change something so that the future works out a different way than it was going to?"

"Only when the time draws near will you know if you can undo what has already happened. Sometimes people die before they are supposed to," said Isabel. "I do not know if Abigail was supposed to die when she did. Some of us are only supposed to be here for a short time. Others, for longer. It might be that no matter what you do, nothing will change."

"Did you die before you were supposed to?" Ravine asked.

"No, Ravine. I was meant to die in the fire. We were all supposed to die in the fire. That is why I had to spend so many years searching."

Ravine was silent for a few moments. Then she asked the question that Isabel was clearly expecting.

"Did Rachel die before she was supposed to?"

Isabel touched Ravine's hands and her eyes softened.

"I know what you want me to say. But Rachel was only supposed to be in your world for a short time. I don't know why some lives are meant to be longer than others. But you lost her when she was supposed to go."

Ravine was silent again, and the two girls sat holding hands, looking at the flowers.

"Ravine, you know how long I waited and searched for someone to help me. It was Rachel who brought you to me."

Ravine wiped away a tear. Isabel stood and reached for Ravine's hand to help her up.

"Hear with your ears, not with your eyes, Ravine. The answers you are seeking are found in the words, not in the pictures Abigail is showing you. Remember, she is showing you what her fears are. Listen carefully to what people are saying. Their actions might mislead you, but their words will be a reliable guide."

Isabel vanished.

Ravine awoke suddenly. It was still dark, and

Isabel's words kept ringing through her head. 'Hear with your ears, not with your eyes ...'

Derek tossed and turned all night. His dreams were full of disturbing images, some that he couldn't understand.

In one image, he could see Ravine lying on stones and dirt, her eyes wide and vacant, her face the colour of mud, and her body perfectly still. A few feet away, Abigail was lying face down in a pool of green murky water, her blonde hair knotted and covered with green slime.

Standing over the two girls was Henry. His eyes were flashing, his hands were clenched, and his smile was wicked. He threw his head back in a sneering laugh. "It's dangerous to play near the well, it's dangerous to play near the well," he cackled.

Derek backed away from the scene, and bumped into a stone wall. He was trapped. Henry turned toward him.

"You can't get away. There ain't nowhere to run," Henry said, laughing uncontrollably.

Derek looked down into the murky water, and at that moment he jolted awake with beads of sweat dripping down the sides of his face.

He sat up and flicked on his night lamp. It took

more than a couple of minutes before his heart rate returned to normal.

"It was Henry," he whispered to himself. "Henry killed Abigail."

Chapter 14

The anticipation of Christmas was in the air. Everywhere you turned, houses were decorated with red plastic bows, and colourful lights. Porches were decorated with gold and green garlands. Inflatable snowmen, painted wooden reindeer, and animated Santas stood on front lawns all over town. Even Mother Nature had cooperated by laying a blanket of snow a couple of inches deep and refreshing it every few days.

Christmas was still almost a month away.

Ravine and Derek had not listened to Madeline's advice. They had continued to pass through the mirror, trying to discover what they were supposed to do. They accepted that her warning was real, and they knew they should pay attention. But the lure of the mirror, and the mystery, were stronger.

"I thought about that, too," Ravine said, as she and Derek walked to school. The snow ploughs had been out, and most people had shoveled the sidewalks, creating banks of snow. Derek and Ravine climbed over the banks, sliding down the larger ones on their bums. "But Isabel's words keep ringing in my ears. Hear with your ears, not with your eyes."

"Well, that would make perfect sense then, wouldn't it?" Derek answered. "Not only do we know how much Henry hates her, but we also heard him telling her to stay away from the well."

But for Ravine, somehow the pieces weren't adding up.

"Why do you think Henry hates her so much?" she asked.

"I don't know," Derek shrugged. "But it is obvious he does. And I saw him in my dream, I saw him push her into the well."

"Did you really see him push her? Or are you just assuming he pushed her? And how do you know it was the well?"

Derek shook his head in frustration. "Same thing," he said. "Henry was there, and Abigail was lying in the pool of water. Where else could it be, if it's not the well? One and one makes two, Ravine."

"Not always Derek," Ravine said.

From here, they watched Sunil and Joannie building a fort out of snow. It hadn't taken long to construct it with all the snow that had fallen over the past week.

Derek and Ravine left their discussion aside, and hurried over to help. Abigail Baldwin was temporarily forgotten.

Ravine started with a small snowball and began to roll it through the piled up snow. Soon Derek and Sunil were at her side, helping her push.

The bell rang out in the school yard, and they left aside the snow fort to get into line.

Annie was already standing at the line, reading a book.

"Have you seen Lisa?" Joannie asked her.

Annie closed her book and shook her head. "No, I thought she was with you."

Before anyone could say anything further, Lisa rushed into line, obviously excited.

"My mom and dad are letting me have a Christmas party! Isn't that great?"

She handed each of her friends a small white envelope, with silver snowflakes stamped in the corners. "It's next Saturday night, and it's formal."

"It's what?" Derek asked, opening his invitation. He read it silently to himself:

Christmas Party Bash.
Ladies wear red. Gentlemen wear black.
Saturday at 6:00 p.m.

Derek refolded his invitation and stuck it in his coat pocket.

"Formal means you guys have to wear a tie, and we ladies wear party dresses," Lisa said.

She turned to Ravine and smiled. Lisa knew that Ravine hated dresses and never wore one.

"I don't have a tie," Derek said, wrinkling his nose.

"And I don't have a dress," Ravine said. She knew Lisa loved to dress up and do fancy things, but a 'formal Christmas party?' That was a bit much.

"I love it!" said Joannie. She turned to Sunil. "Do you have a tie?"

"Yeah, I needed one to wear to my Grampa's funeral last year."

"Come on, guys. It sounds like fun," Annie said, half smiling.

"You bet it's going to be fun!" Lisa exclaimed. "My mom and dad booked a carriage ride through the centre of town and all round the park so we can look at all the Christmas lights. And the best part is that the carriage will be pulled by four horses!"

"That's cool," they all said in chorus, almost like they had practiced it. Even Ravine. The dressing up part did not sound like much fun to her, but the horses and the carriage sure did. Maybe she could endure wearing a dress for one night. After all, it was only a dress. How bad could it be?

Of course, that meant she'd have to get a dress first.

The last bell rang, and as they shuffled into school, they all continued chatting about next Saturday and the horse drawn carriage. But Ravine's mind was only half interested. Even with all the excitement, Isabel's words echoed quietly through Ravine's head. "Hear with your ears, not with your eyes."

Ravine showed her mother the invitation when she got home from school.

"Oh, Ravine! We'll have to go shopping for dresses," she said, clapping her hands together. She looked like she had just won a lottery.

Ravine knew her mother would be delighted. She hadn't worn a dress since Rachel's funeral, and she couldn't remember if she had ever worn one before then.

Throughout supper, Ravine listened half-heartedly as her mother chattered about dresses, dress shops, and then more dresses. And then more shops. Her father said nothing, and Ravine was sure this excited him about as much as it excited her.

It had been a while since Ravine's mother had been this animated about anything, so she guessed she was happy that her mother was so pleased. But she still didn't want to wear a dress. She was actually quite annoyed with Lisa for making this a formal party. Shame on her, she thought miserably. Shame on her.

After supper, Ravine headed to her room feeling exhausted. Listening to her mother had worn her down. Why were her parents always trying to change her into something she wasn't? She wasn't Rachel. Her sister had always liked dressing up in prissy things. But she didn't, and she hated that everyone seemed to think she should.

As she shut her bedroom door, she thought about the only dress she could remember wearing. Rachel's funeral seemed like a lifetime ago, now. On the day of the funeral, she had sat on her bed staring at the black dress hanging on her closet door. She always thought of Rachel in a dress, and as she waited to go to the funeral home, she could picture Rachel twirling around in the dress she would soon be putting on herself.

"Look at how beautiful it is, Ravine," she would have said.

But Rachel was a pretty girl, with long legs that her mother called ballerina legs. Her dark brown hair was beautiful, and it hung down her back with the bounce and shine of a shampoo commercial. Rachel looked a lot like Ravine, but more girly. And definitely prettier, Ravine thought.

Tonight, she sat on her bed thinking of her younger sister.

"I wonder what you would have looked like at my age," she said out loud. "I bet you would have become a dancer. You were always so good, and so delicate." She wondered if Rachel would have played sports, like her. Ravine was sure she knew the answers. They might have looked alike, but they were very different.

"I guess it doesn't matter anymore," Ravine said softly.

Finally, Ravine turned her attention to the mirror. Abigail's reflection flickered in and out of focus, so she got off the bed and moved closer to the glass.

Abigail reached her arm out, but Ravine backed away. She wanted to go through the mirror. She wanted to solve the mystery of Abigail Baldwin. But what if she didn't come back this time? What if this time she was trapped forever?

Her heart pounded loudly at that thought. But

Abigail kept motioning her closer, enticing her with a friendly smile.

Then, without any further hesitation, Ravine reached for Abigail's hand, and she disappeared through the glass.

Ravine opened her eyes. The sun shining through the window cast a shadow on the wall behind her of a horse bent over a bale of hay. The smell of fresh dung and ammonia filled her nostrils, and Ravine's eyes began to water. She stood up slowly, brushing straw from her shirt and picking pieces of straw out of her hair. It was itchy and she noticed scratches on her bare legs. Stepping onto the concrete floor she heard a scritching sound coming from one of the further stalls.

She walked by two horse stalls, stopping at the third. She found herself gazing up into the eyes of a large white speckled horse. Curious with the stranger in front of him, he stopped chewing the hay that was hanging half out of his mouth and eyed Ravine up and down. She had been horseback riding before, so she instinctively offered her hand for sniffing. But she pulled it away quickly, realizing she had nothing to offer.

The horse stretched his neck further through the iron bars, trying to sniff the girl in front of him.

Ravine suddenly realized that this horse could see and smell her, when no one else but Abigail could.

"Can you hear me too?" she asked.

The horse whinnied in response.

Ravine left the horse, and headed toward the sunshine. She passed out through the barn doors, and from here she could faintly hear a male voice in the distance. She walked around the barn and the voice became louder as she got closer to the side where the pasture began.

It was Henry, and he was busy brushing Gent. Ravine walked toward him as Henry continued chattering away to the horse.

"I don't know why she doesn't like me, Gent. She's always so mean and so bossy." He kept brushing the horse's hair in long even strokes. He gave Gent a few apple slices. "I wish I didn't like her so much."

Ravine was surprised to hear Henry say that. She knew he was talking about Abigail.

"You like me, don't you Gent?" Henry went on. "You don't think I was raised in a barn, do you?" Then he chuckled. "I guess you'd probably like me better if I was."

He continued to groom Gent.

"I always thought she'd be the girl I'd want to marry. She's so pretty, and so smart. I wish I was as smart as her."

Ravine stood in awe, her mouth wide open. Henry didn't hate Abigail; he was in love with her. He was angry because Abigail didn't feel the same way. Watching Henry now, Ravine knew that it couldn't have been Henry who killed Abigail. At least not on purpose.

Derek must have it all wrong.

Three more days until Lisa's Christmas bash.

When Ravine got home from school her mother was in a mood. A dress shopping mood.

"Let's go to the city and get something nice for you to wear on Saturday," her mother said. She was stacking the dishwasher and obviously excited about taking Ravine shopping.

Ravine smiled and nodded meekly. There was no point in arguing. Ravine really did want to go to the party, and she knew the only way she could was if she had a dress. So her mother was going to win this battle.

Ravine would arrive at Lisa's party in a dress. But she didn't have to like it.

Ravine stood outside the change room in a fiery red dress that hung past her knees. She thought it was complimented nicely by her baseball cap and the white socks pulled up over her calves. Maybe for a formal occasion, I have to turn the hat so the brim is at the front, she mused.

She peered at her reflection in the mirror. It had been a while, she thought, since she last looked in a mirror and saw only herself.

Her mom pulled the ball cap off her head.

"Now that's so much better, sweetheart."

"I look ridiculous," Ravine pouted.

"Of course you don't. I think it looks beautiful on you."

Her mother was smiling. "You should really wear dresses more often. You look so pretty."

Ravine crossed her arms and turned to face her mother.

"Okay, let's buy a couple just for school."

"Really?"

"No, not really, Mom. Dresses are stupid. Other girls might like them, but I don't. Some girls even look good in them, but I don't. It's not me. I'm not Rachel."

She stopped almost as soon as she said it.

"I'm sorry, Mom. I didn't mean that. I just …"

"It's okay, Ravine. I understand."

After a moment of awkward silence, Ravine looked at herself in the mirror again.

"Well, maybe it doesn't look so bad," she said.

"But I really was kidding about wearing dresses to school. Seriously, no one would recognize me."

"If you don't like this style, you can try something else," her mother offered, ignoring Ravine's sarcasm.

Stomping back into the change room, Ravine was loud. "Of course," she said. "Of course, I want to try on another dress. Why don't I try on all of them? This is torture," she said, as she whipped the dress over the door. "Why don't you just kill me? It would have to feel better than this!"

There was silence on the other side of the door. The quiet hit Ravine harder than anything her mother could have said. How could she be such an idiot? She'd already made that stupid crack about Rachel. What was she thinking?

She peeked her head out. "I'm sorry, mom. Really, I didn't mean it. I'm not being very nice tonight, am I?"

Her mother stared at her momentarily, but then melted into a soft smile.

"Of course you didn't mean it, dear. I know this makes you uncomfortable. But wait until everybody sees how pretty you are going to look. Now hurry up and change. We still have to find you a nice pair of shoes. I'm sure you know that running shoes and your ball cap aren't going to match the dress," she said with a chuckle.

At the same time that Ravine was being tortured in the dress shop, Derek was being dragged around a department store. Danielle hovered a few steps behind their mother, speaking quietly on her cell phone.

He didn't mind about having to get dressed up, so he wasn't putting up nearly so much fuss as Ravine. But he hated shopping.

"Just a tie, Mom. That's all I need. Any tie will do."

He groaned as he looked at the display of ties. There were hundreds of them. Who knew there were so many different kinds? And some of those colours were really wild. Who would wear stuff like this, he was thinking.

"We can't just get you a tie, Derek. You're going to need a nice pair of pants and a dress shirt. And we should probably get a blazer to go along with it. This is supposed to be a formal party."

His mother wandered over to a display rack full of pants.

"How about these?" she asked. She held up a pair of pleated black trousers. Before he could answer, she grabbed a white dress shirt and then headed to the tie racks. She quickly picked out three or four, and then walked over to the jackets.

She's like a shopping machine, Derek thought to himself, as he watched her quickly choose a dark grey herringbone blazer.

"Here, this will all look nice together," she said. "Try on the pants, shirt, and jacket, honey. Then we can decide which is the best tie."

Derek made a disgusted face, but he grabbed the clothes from his mother and went into the change room. The sooner he got changed, the sooner this would be over.

He disappeared behind the swinging door

When he finally emerged, his mother was delighted.

"You look wonderful. Danielle, look at your brother. Doesn't he look handsome?"

Danielle tucked her phone into her purse.

"Yes, Mother he does," she smirked. "A very handsome penguin."

A few more minutes to decide on a tie, and they were done and on their way home. Derek was brooding in the front seat of the car; Danielle was in the back looking at all the Christmas decorations as they drove past.

When they got home, Danielle got out of the car

first, muttering under her breath again about the handsome penguin.

Two more days until Lisa's Christmas bash.

Derek and Ravine sat on her bed as Abigail watched them through the mirror.

"I'm telling you, Derek, Henry is in love with Abigail," said Ravine.

Derek shook his head. "That can't be. First, remember how he talks to her. You've heard him. He's rude and ignorant. And second, he's Abigail's cousin. Henry killed her. It's that simple," he finished, shaking his head again.

"They are not real cousins, Derek," Ravine said. She ignored Derek's last comment. "Abe isn't Abigail's real father, and Henry is Abe's nephew. So Abigail and Henry aren't related."

Derek sat in silence, obviously thinking about this.

"I don't care. I'm still convinced he killed Abigail."

They sat in silence staring at their reflections, lost in their own thoughts.

But Abigail kept waving to them, beckoning them to join her.

"My mom took me dress shopping," Ravine

said. "It was horrible. I don't want to go to
pid party and wear that stupid dress."

only for one night, and then you never have
to wear it again."

"It's easy for you to say, you don't have to wear
a dress."

She turned to Derek and glared at him.

"Well, I was going to wear a dress," he said.

"Very funny."

"But my mom decided I had to wear a jacket
and tie instead. Danielle says I look like a penguin.
I hate to admit it, but she's right."

Ravine sat brooding. "You won't laugh at me,
will you?"

"Geez, Ravine, it's only a dress. Of course I won't
laugh at you."

They sat for a while longer, gazing absently at
Abigail inside the mirror

"What colour dress were you going to get,
Derek?"

They both laughed. Derek stood up and walked
toward the mirror. "What happened to you?" he
whispered.

Ravine got up and joined him.

"Well, I guess the only way to find out …" She
let the sentence hang in the air.

Derek took Ravine's hand. He could feel her tremble slightly as they stepped closer to Abigail.

"On the count of three, okay?"

They held tight to each other's hand.

Derek counted. "One … two …"

"THREE!" they said together.

They stepped toward the mirror and reached their free hands toward Abigail. Derek and Ravine pushed on the glass. Nothing happened. Their hearts were pounding madly.

They pushed again, harder this time, and a few seconds later they passed through the glass and vanished.

Chapter 15

Derek and Ravine watched the festivities taking place before them. A few people were gathered in the small living room. They meandered through the crowd, as if they were part of the celebration.

"I wonder what's in here?" Abigail sat on the rocking chair, holding a brown package to her ear. She shook it endlessly. Derek and Ravine had never seen any of the other people, except for Henry, Meredith, and Abe. Most of the strangers were much older than Abigail.

Meredith smiled as the string fell to the floor.

It was Abigail's birthday, and Ravine wondered if these guests were related to Abigail. There was one who looked to be about the same age, but all the rest were adults. Ravine wondered where Abigail's friends were. She looked at Derek who was darting his eyes from one guest to another.

Abigail gasped, "Oh, Mama, I can't believe it. Thank you so much!"

She carefully placed the leather book on her lap and opened to the first page. Reading out loud for everyone, "*Oliver Twist; or, the Parish Boy's Progress*, by Charles Dickens." She thumbed through the pages, silently reading words here and there.

"Aunt Agatha and I thought you might like it," said her mother.

"That's right. That's what your mama told me," said a large lady in a soft green dress. She wore white gloves that looked out of place in this modest home. "I thought a nice new dress, or shoes, but Meredith assured me you would like this more."

Abigail was obviously excited. She ran her fingers along the spine of the book, feeling the soft leather. She held it up and touched it to her cheek, sniffing the newness of the binding.

Last year, Abigail told everyone, Miss Blakeney had read aloud to her students another book by Charles Dickens. It had taken the whole school year, and she had read it a chapter at a time. She said that was the way it was originally published, in a monthly magazine.

"I really enjoyed that story. And even the name of it would make anybody want to know what it was about. It was called *The Personal History,*

Adventures, Experience and Observation of David Copperfield the Younger of Blunderstone Rookery (which he never meant to publish on any account). Miss Blakeney said everyone just called it *David Copperfield*, but I like the long title better."

Ravine whispered to Derek, "They're making a pretty big deal out of a book."

"Look around. Do you see any other books? You can't imagine how expensive that must have been, and what it means to them. They don't have much money. I'll bet that's a few months' earnings right there."

Abe handed Abigail another present. This time, the brown package was much smaller and fit nicely into the palm of her hand. She slowly peeled off the wrapping to expose a black wooden box. She paused and looked at Abe.

"Go ahead," he encouraged. "Open it up."

She lifted the lid and gasped. She carefully took out a gold chain and dangled it between her fingers.

"Oh, Abe. It's beautiful!"

There was a pendant hanging from the chain, and Abigail traced the word engraved on the pendant with her finger: Abby.

"It's exquisite," Meredith exclaimed. "I had no idea you were getting her something like that."

"It really is a beauty," Abe replied. "But it isn't from me. You know the saddle was from me."

He turned toward Henry whose face burned red.

"Uncle Abe helped me pick it out. I saved all my monies. I thought it would look nice on you, Abby. I know you always wear the locket with your papa's picture, but I thought this might look nice with it."

He stared at his feet. His ears had turned the same shade of red as his face.

For a moment Abigail was quiet. Then she stood up and leaned over to kiss Henry on the cheek.

"It's beautiful, Henry. Would you help me put it on?"

Everybody clapped and wished Abigail a happy birthday. Then Meredith started to get out the food she had prepared last night after Abigail went to bed.

Abigail stood up on a chair and waved to get everyone's attention. "I want to thank everybody for making this day so special. I want to thank Henry for the beautiful necklace. And I want to thank my parents for everything they give me every day. I love you all!"

It was probably only Derek who noticed, but he saw Abe's face melt in contentment. He knew instinctively that this was probably the first time Abigail had referred to Abe as one of her parents.

Derek walked home with his head down. He opened the front door, and as it slammed behind him, he could hear his mother yelling to him from the living room.

"Is that you, Derek?"

Derek walked into the living room and sat beside her.

"What's wrong? Did you and Ravine have a fight?"

"No, why do you ask?"

Danielle was talking on the phone, but still managed to stick out her tongue at him in between words. Now that's a talent, he thought.

"Well, you just went over fifteen minutes ago, and now you're back and by the look of it, you aren't too happy."

Derek looked at his watch. His mother was right. The mirror was exactly like Isabel's house. Every time they went into her house, time stood still. Travelling through the mirror was the same.

"No, we didn't have a fight. Ravine remembered she had some homework she needed to get done," he lied.

"And what about you? Do you have homework to get done?"

"No, I finished it at school."

Derek sat for a few minutes, and then went upstairs to his bedroom. Closing the door behind him, he flopped down on the bed with his basketball. All he could think about was Henry. He was so sure it must have been Henry who killed Abigail, but the Henry they had seen before didn't fit with the one they saw today at Abigail's birthday party. Now he wasn't so sure anymore.

Ravine was right. Henry didn't hate Abigail at all.

Tossing the basketball up at the ceiling, he thought that none of this makes any sense. Nothing about Abigail was any more clear than when they first learned about her.

One more day until Lisa's Christmas bash.

Ravine rushed into school ten minutes late. She was already unzipping her jacket as she pulled on the front door handle. She headed straight to the office and waited in line behind a few grade eight kids she recognized. They were all there to get their late slips from the secretary. As she waited, she took off her hat and mittens, shoving them into her backpack.

Then she wiped her glasses that had fogged up as soon as she entered the warm building.

After Mrs. Dackery handed her the late slip, and gave her the expected lecture about punctuality, Ravine ran down the hall dragging her coat on the floor behind her. She quickly changed out of her boots, stuffing them against the wall among all the other boots. She slipped on her indoor shoes, without bothering to tie them, hung her jacket on Sandy's hook instead of her own, and tried ever so quietly to open the door to her classroom. Forty-six eyes looked up from their books. Two eyes looked from the front of the room.

Without a word, Ravine sat down at her desk. It wasn't long before she got notes passed from Joannie and Derek. She discreetly set them on her lap and unfolded Derek's first.

'Where were you this morning? Why are you so late?'

Being as careful as she could, so she wouldn't get caught, she wrote back.

'I left early to go see Madeline. I didn't think I would be there so long.'

She passed the note back to Derek.

A few seconds later, a kick on her chair told her the note was coming back. Ravine leaned back to get it.

'Why? Why did you go there?'

She replied, 'To see if she could talk to Rachel for me. She said she could, but Rachel would appear when the time was right. Whatever that means. I'll tell you later.'

She slipped the note back to Derek and then unfolded Joannie's. 'Did you get your dress? Aren't you excited for Saturday? I can't wait! You should see the dress my mom bought me!'

The note went on to describe Joannie's dress and Ravine just rolled her eyes. She decided not to respond. Her stomach twisted in tight knots, and she wondered if there was any way she could get out of going to this party.

Derek read Ravine's note. He knew she still thought of Rachel often, but he thought if she could just let go, maybe she would be happier. He hoped Madeline might be able to help her see that.

He folded up the note and stuck it in his binder. Then he went back to listening to Mrs. MacDonald, who was explaining the effects of erosion. Derek was always interested in science, so he read a lot about it himself. He already knew about erosion, so Mrs. McDonald wasn't very interesting at the moment. She was going on and on about how the wind and the snow and the rain eventually wore everything down.

If she doesn't stop, he thought, I'm going to erode before this morning is over.

They didn't get a chance to talk at recess or lunch, because all their friends wanted to talk about what they were wearing to Lisa's party. Derek and Ravine were quiet because that didn't interest them at all.

On the way home from school, Ravine was finally able to tell Derek about her conversation with Madeline.

"She is the coolest person ever," Ravine stated. "She said that, eventually, I will be able to communicate with her. I just need more practice."

"Communicate with who?"

Derek hunkered deeper into his jacket as the wind picked up. It was a warm jacket, but he was cold all the same.

"Rachel! Who else?"

Derek stopped and took hold of Ravine's arm. He looked at her, trying to be as comforting as he knew how to be.

"She's dead, Ravine," he said simply.

"I realize that. I was there when it happened. I was there when we put her coffin in the ground and covered it with dirt. I know she's dead. But there are people who can communicate with the dead, Derek, and Madeline thinks I have that ability. I just need to … what were the exact words she said? Oh, yeah. I need to hone my ability."

"What is that supposed to mean?"

Ravine shrugged. "I don't know. But I'm going to find out."

They continued on in silence for a couple of blocks until Derek spoke again.

"What difference is it going to make, Ravine, if you can communicate with her? It's not going to bring her back."

"I know. But I just want to say goodbye."

The rest of the way home was quiet, except for the sound of the wind that was blowing even stronger now. The snow on the streets muffled the sounds of the few cars that passed them.

As they got to their houses, Ravine turned to say goodbye, but stopped.

"Derek, you need to blow your nose."

Chapter 16

"It's hideous!" Ravine yelled into the receiver, staring at herself in the mirror. The red silky dress hung about half way down her calves, and it sparkled brightly with the sequins woven through the bodice.

"I'm sure you look fine. Geez, Ravine. How bad can it be? Girls wear dresses all the time!"

"Other girls, maybe, but not me! Shame on Lisa! Shame on her!" she yelled uncontrollably.

Derek couldn't help but laugh. "Calm down. It's only for one night. Nobody's gonna laugh at you. I'm sure you'll look just fine. Do you want my mom to drive us?"

He was standing in front of a mirror himself, thinking he was looking pretty good! Not too bad, he thought to himself. Definitely a handsome penguin.

He was wearing his new black pants and white

shirt. He had convinced his mother to get him a Philadelphia Flyers tie because it would match the pants and shirt nicely. He didn't care that it looked out of place with the herringbone jacket; he looked cool. He almost went for the Pittsburgh tie, especially after Danielle said he looked like a penguin. But he decided he liked the Philly colours better.

Looking down at his feet, he frowned at the black, nicely polished dress shoes. There was nothing cool about that. But the rest of him looked good.

"No! I'll meet you at her house," Ravine said, pouting at her reflection in the mirror. She was so upset about all of this that she didn't even notice Abigail wasn't there to look back at her. All she knew was that she looked like a freak. In fact, she looked like a sparkly version of Clifford the Big Red Dog. With glasses. This night was going to be horrible.

"You better not chicken out," Derek said.

There was no way he wanted to miss this. He didn't really pay attention to the way Ravine was dressed at Rachel's funeral, he was sad about her too. He liked Ravine's little sister, but he was far more concerned at the time about Ravine. This time, he was going to be paying attention. Heck, solar eclipses happened more often than this.

n't chicken out. I said I'll be there, and I'll
."

She hung up the phone in anger and turned
sideways to look in the mirror again. She should
just stay home. She was sure she had seen something
that looked like this in some horror movie.

Her hair was much too frizzy, her dress was
much too bright, and her face was much too pale.
She threw on her baseball cap. Much better, she
thought, although the colour doesn't really match
the awful dress.

Then she pulled out the new shoes her mother
had made her try on. They were patent leather, and
they looked to her like shiny black slippers with
narrow heels. The heels were only about an inch
high, but all she ever wore was running shoes. So
when she slipped her feet into them and tried to
walk, she wobbled back and forth unsteadily.

For crying out loud, she thought. Why would
anyone wear stuff like this if they didn't have to?
It was like walking on slippers with nails sticking
out the bottom of the heels. It can't be possible to
balance on these things. How do girls walk in these
things? Why do they want to? This is nuts.

She stumbled out of her room, and then
stumbled toward the stairs. She held tightly to the
railing, and carefully placed one foot in front of

her. Okay so far. Then the second step. Still good. But she lost her balance before she could make it to the third, and went tumbling down the stairs on her bum. The thudding and bumping echoed throughout the house.

"What was that?"

Her mother came rushing through the kitchen door with Ravine's father right behind her.

"Are you okay, honey?"

Ravine looked up. She had left one shoe near the top of the stairs, and tears were running down her cheeks.

"No, I'm not okay, Mom. Do I look like I'm okay?"

Her father helped her up and then went to retrieve her other shoe.

"This could have happened to anyone, Ravine. I am sure you are not the first girl to have fallen down the stairs. Nor will you be the last," her father said.

He held out her shoe to her, but she could see the look in his eyes.

"Don't you dare laugh at me," she cried.

Her father said of course he wouldn't laugh, but he left the room quickly all the same. Just in case.

Ravine wiped away her tears as her mother led her into the kitchen.

"Girls don't wear baseball caps with dresses." She removed the cap as she sat Ravine down at the kitchen table. "There, that's better."

Her mother plugged in a curling iron. "Now, your hair is beautiful. But we can make it even nicer."

As the curling iron warmed, her mother took out a small plastic container filled with hair clips. Ravine groaned. This was going to be a really, really long night.

Ravine felt like this was taking forever, and started fidgeting. Her mother told her to sit still, but the longer it took, the harder that was.

When she was finally finished, her mother handed Ravine a mirror. She didn't recognize herself.

"I don't like it," she said, pouting.

"You look beautiful. What's not to like?"

"It doesn't look like me. It looks like someone else altogether."

"Sure it looks like you, honey. It's just a different version of you, that's all."

She kissed Ravine on the forehead and told her to get ready to leave.

Ravine stood at Lisa's front door, staring at it. Just ring the stupid doorbell, she said to herself.

It's just one night. You'll survive, and then you can work real hard to forget about it.

She slowly lifted her hand, and closed her eyes as she pressed the bell quickly, before she changed her mind.

"You look lovely, Ravine," Lisa's mother said, as she opened the door. "Everybody's downstairs. Let me take your coat."

Ravine slowly walked to the stairs, and she could see all her friends downstairs, joking around. She started down the stairs, being as careful as she could. Sunil saw her first.

"Ravine's here!"

Everyone stopped what they were doing, and Ravine walked down to meet them. She tried not to look at anyone. She needed to concentrate on going down the stairs in her stupid shoes.

As she stepped off the last stair, safely, she saw Derek looking at her with his mouth wide open.

"Wow, Ravine. You look like a Barbie doll!"

He cursed himself silently. What a stupid, stupid thing to say. But all of a sudden he was tongue-tied. He had never seen Ravine look so much like a … well, like a girl.

"What did you say?" she said, getting close to his face. "Take it back!"

"I'm sorry. That didn't come out right. I meant

it as a compliment!" he said defensively. "You look really nice," he managed to spit out.

"Oh. Okay, then."

Before that could go any further, Sunil suddenly piped up, although it was hard to hear what he said with his mouth crammed full of potato chips.

"Hey, when are we going on the carriage ride?"

It was a perfect night for a carriage ride.

Lisa's father had arranged for the carriage to take them through the centre of town, the park, and along the river where the big old houses had such beautiful displays of Christmas lights.

It was an old fashioned carriage, drawn by four horses, and big enough to hold eight passengers. Snow was falling lightly, even though most of the sky was clear and full of stars.

Lisa's dad had the driver stop the carriage in the park, pulling the horses up to the river that meandered through town. It wouldn't be long before the river was frozen over for the winter, but it was still flowing strong right now.

Lisa's father gave each of the kids Christmas crackers and a small present. Then he stood them in front of the river to snap a few pictures. He said he would make sure that he got copies of the photos for all of them.

Back at Lisa's house, her mother had a late supper of take-out pizza waiting for them. While they were eating, they all popped the Christmas crackers and opened the small gift Lisa's dad had given them. They turned out to be Christmas picture frames.

The party ended just before midnight, and Derek's mother came to get him and Ravine.

Ravine and Derek chatted non-stop in the back seat about Lisa's great party. Ravine had forgotten all about how horrible tonight was going to be. When Derek's mom stopped the car in Ravine's driveway, Ravine opened the door and Derek turned to her.

"You really do look nice in a dress. You should wear them more often."

Ravine snorted. "It's a good thing you'll have a picture of this, because you'll never see it again!"

She slammed the car door and ran happily up the front steps. Over the course of the evening, she had figured out to walk in those stupid shoes. She opened the front door, letting it slam behind her. She knew her parents were going to be waiting up for her, so she headed straight to the living room.

They were sitting on the couch waiting, and she sat down to tell them all about the party. She showed them her gift and told them about how much fun the carriage ride was. She chatted happily about her evening until twelve thirty, when her parents sent her off to bed.

She was going to tell her mother that she guessed she didn't really look so bad in a dress after all, but decided not to.

Inside her room, alone with Abigail, Ravine couldn't sleep. Imagine, she thought. Derek actually said she looked nice in a dress. And Lisa and Joannie really liked her dress. And they thought she looked wonderful. She guessed it wasn't so bad after all, but it still didn't seem right for her to be wearing a dress. It wasn't her. It was someone else.

She got up to look in the mirror, ignoring Abigail's smiling face. Yes, it was someone else. This is what Rachel would have looked like at my age, she thought.

She looked at herself one last time before undressing. Smiling, she took the clips out of her hair, letting it fall past her shoulders. Maybe tomorrow she'd wear it that way, instead of her usual ponytail. Maybe.

Ravine climbed into bed, pulling the covers to her chin. She stared at Abigail. What would it have been like to live back then, she wondered, when girls always wore dresses. Before falling asleep, she looked at the crumpled dress thrown on the floor and happily thought of her night.

Ravine tossed and turned for a while. Images of Abigail running and laughing drifted through her mind. The smell of daisies filled her nose, and she could feel the green grass, soft beneath her bare feet. But that soon passed, and she entered a very peaceful sleep.

Derek opened the fridge. Leftover ham, cheese, an unopened package of bologna. He moved the milk, but nothing good was hiding behind it. He shut the door and settled for a peanut butter sandwich. At least it would stop the rumbling until morning. Why am I so hungry, he wondered? I just spent most of the last five hours nibbling on snacks and eating pizza.

In his room, he closed the door and turned on the desk lamp. As he ate his sandwich, he stared at the unopened letter, still lying on his desk. He wished his mother had just thrown it out, that she had never given it to him. She hadn't asked about it since.

He remembered that she said it was up to him what he did with the letter. She would talk to him about it if he wanted, or he could just ignore it. But sooner or later he would have to face it. He couldn't hide forever.

Now he sat spinning the letter with his fore finger. Opening this letter would be like opening a can of worms, Derek thought to himself.

"Yucky, green slimy ones," he said out loud.

And why should I anyway? What difference would it make?

"Probably none," he said, speaking out loud again.

He got up and changed into his pajama bottoms. His life was great just the way it was. There was no need to go and complicate everything now.

"This will just make everything worse," he said. Derek stared at the envelope. Why hadn't his mother just thrown it out? Why did she have to ruin everything by giving it to him?

He grabbed the envelope and turned off his desk lamp. He got into bed and turned on his bedside lamp. It sure is thick, Derek thought to himself.

"I'm surprised there is so much to say."

Why am I talking out loud, he thought. There's nobody here to listen.

After all this time, what can there be to say? Maybe if the letter had come a few years ago, things might have been different. But not now. He wondered if a letter had come for Danielle as well.

He threw the unopened letter on the night table and turned off the light.

Chapter 17

Ravine's peaceful sleep only lasted a couple of hours before her tossing and turning woke her. She twisted her head to look at the clock. Only a little past three. Everything was dark and still, except for her mirror.

She turned to face Abigail. It was hard to see her clearly in the dark room, but a soft blue-green glow illuminated the outer edges of her reflection. Without thinking, Ravine sat up and swung her legs out from the warm covers. The floor was cold and it sent a tiny chill throughout her body. In a groggy, lack-of-sleep haze, she walked toward Abigail.

Ravine pushed hard against the cold smooth glass. Each time it seemed to be taking longer to pass through. Finally, it softened like pushing on a balloon that was losing air, and suddenly she slipped through into Abigail's world.

"You shouldn't sit so close to the hole. It's dangerous!"

Abigail turned and saw Henry looking down at her. He looked like an angel as the sun was directly behind his head. But she could see his frowning face, and she recognized the growl in his voice. Abigail turned back toward the hole, not moving.

Henry sat down beside her.

"Why did you give me such a beautiful necklace, Henry?" She turned to face him.

Henry remained quiet as he peered down the dark hole.

"I thought you didn't like me," she went on. "It's an odd gift to give someone you don't like."

Ravine approached them from behind and sat down beside Abigail, who turned and smiled at her.

"Who said I didn't like you?"

Henry's ears turned pink. He was looking directly at Ravine, but she wasn't there, in his eyes.

Abigail looked into Henry's eyes. His long, brown curly hair was highlighted with honey strands, bleached from working long hours in the summer sun. His bronzed skin and his dimples made him look boyish and playful, when he wasn't trying to look angry.

"Well, Henry Adams, it is the best birthday present I have ever received." She hesitated, then added, "and I'm glad it came from you."

Henry's cheeks turned pink to match his ears. His dark eyes were twinkling.

"I'm glad it came from me, too."

Tentatively, he took Abigail's hand, and they sat together, silently looking down into the dark hole.

Derek awoke in a strange panic. His heart was beating quickly, beads of sweat appeared on his cheeks, and for a moment he didn't know where he was. He sat up in bed, looking around his bedroom. The pale light of nearly-dawn snuck gently through the window, and Derek laid back down.

He covered himself up and rolled over. It was too early to get up. He closed his eyes and tried to get back to sleep, but his heart continued to pound loudly. He tried to ignore it.

Abigail and Henry walked toward the house holding hands. Through the screen door, Ravine could see Meredith sitting at the kitchen table, while Abe stood beside her pouring a cup of tea. Her eyes looked red and puffy.

"Little Fredrick was up all night crying. I tried everything I know to settle him, but nothing worked.

I can't believe you and Abigail didn't hear him. The sun was just starting to rise when he finally fell asleep, probably not more than fifteen minutes before you got up. I'm not sure when you got out of bed, because as soon as he stopped crying, I fell asleep myself."

Abe sat down across from Meredith and offered her the cup of tea.

They both looked up as Abigail and Henry came through the door, and looked at each other in surprise as they saw Henry was holding Abigail's hand. They both knew enough not to say anything about it.

Ravine was standing very close to Abigail. Until now, her body had always felt light and airy whenever she came to Abigail's world. She had always felt like an image, a picture, a reflection. But lately, when she traveled through the mirror, she noticed a tingling sensation in her fingertips. Now, Ravine could feel that tingling sensation slowly travelling up her arms.

Abe put two more cups on the table, and sat down again. Henry poured, Abigail's first, and then his own. Ravine couldn't help but see the look that was exchanged between Meredith and Abe.

"Oh, Meredith," Abe said, returning to their

earlier conversation. "Things will get better, you'll see."

Just then, a wail came from the cradle and Meredith laid her heavy head on the table. Ravine thought she could see tears of exhaustion trickle from Meredith's eyes.

"I'll get him," Abe said

When Abe returned from the other room, Fredrick was swaddled in a blanket. His little chubby face was red from crying.

"Abigail, how would you like to take your brother for a walk? You can see your mama is very tired."

"Of course."

Abe handed the baby to Abigail, and disappeared outside to fetch the buggy.

"I'll come along and keep you company, if you don't mind," Henry said.

Abigail smiled and said that would be very nice.

As Ravine walked outside beside Abigail and Henry, she noticed a strange force that she hadn't felt before. It felt like some kind of energy connecting her to Abigail, almost like an invisible rope, but one made out of energy. She didn't really know what she meant by that, but it seemed to her to be the best way to describe it.

The force seemed to want her to go along with Abigail, but she stood still, trying to fight the feeling of being dragged along. She could now feel that strange tingling sensation in her fingers and arms was also in her feet.

Ravine hurried back into the house as Henry and Abigail walked further into the distance. It took all of Ravine's strength to separate herself from Abigail. As she climbed the stairs toward the mirror in the loft, she could feel the heaviness of her body and the sweet smell of daisies.

She stood in front of the mirror, feeling that she needed to get back home. At the same time, there was a strong desire in her to stay. Nothing was making sense to her.

She leaned against the mirror, trying to fight the urge to run after Abigail. When she didn't immediately pass through, she pushed harder.

What if she never got back? What if she never saw Derek again? Or her family?

Before, getting home always happened abruptly, like someone was pushing her back to her own world. But now it was if that someone wanted her to stay.

The tingling in Ravine's body became more and more intense the harder she pushed on the glass. It had now spread beyond her hands and feet, and her whole body tingled. How long had she been standing here? Minutes? Hours? Her body was beginning to feel real. For a split second, she could feel her arms and legs. She flickered in and out of focus.

She closed her eyes, trying to make sense out of what was happening. A few more hard pushes against the glass, but nothing happened. The reflection gazing back at her now looked scared and small. She could see herself flickering in and out of focus.

The flickering.

The pins and needles.

The flickering.

Exhausted, Ravine finally gave up. The mirror was locked. The portal between her world and Abigail's had finally broken down. It was just as Madeline had said. Ravine backed away from the mirror and stood still for a few moments.

The flickering.

The pins and needles.

The flickering.

Then she climbed down the ladder and ran out the door to try and catch up to Abigail and Henry. The pins and needles continued. More intense now. Ravine's feet burned and she was having a hard time running.

ickering.

Ravine followed down the gravel path that ran in front of Abigail's house. Her whole body felt as if it were on fire. The pins and needles continued, this time starting at the very top of her head and travelling down to the ends of her toes. Her whole body hurt with an intense pain she had never felt before.

Flickering.

Henry and Abigail were on their way back from walking the baby. They were heading toward her.

Finally, the pins and needles stopped.

"Abigail!"

Ravine yelled and raced toward the girl. As Abigail approached, she could see the distress on Ravine's face.

The look in Abigail's eyes asked what was wrong. As Ravine shook her head, trying to catch her breath, Henry spoke.

"Who's your friend, Abby?"

Derek jolted awake, sweating, and sat up straight. His heart was pounding loudly, like he had been running real hard. Something was very wrong, and he had a sense of fear.

He climbed out of bed and got dressed, unable to shake the feeling of terror

He knew he was the last one getting up this morning, and headed downstairs to the kitchen. His sister was talking on the phone, naturally, and his mother was busy with some baking.

"Well good morning, sir. If you hadn't gotten up in another five minutes, I was coming up there to drag you out of bed."

Her voice sounded muffled because she had her head poked in the oven as she spoke.

"What are you up to today?"

Derek grabbed a piece of fruit, and noticed his hand was shaking. He didn't seem to be able to stop it.

"I'm going over to Ravine's," he replied. "Okay?"

"Of course it is."

He started to get his boots and jacket on, but his mother insisted he needed more for breakfast than just a piece of fruit.

"There's still some toast being kept warm in the toaster oven," she said.

Derek took piece of toast and started to eat. He didn't even bother with butter, or jam, or peanut butter. When he was done, he finished getting dressed and headed out the door, letting it slam behind him.

Something was not right, and he started to run

to Ravine's. The sidewalks were icy and he slipped a couple of times, once falling flat on his stomach. He braced himself for the fall, crushing the banana that was still in his hand.

He climbed the steps to Ravine's verandah and rang the bell.

No answer.

He rang it again and waited. Still no answer.

So he rang four or five times in a row.

Nothing.

He tried the door handle, but it was locked.

He thought about going home to ask his mother for the key, but that would mean an explanation, and he couldn't give one. He didn't know why it was so important for him to get into Ravine's house right now; he just knew it was.

He ran around to the back of the house. He jiggled the handle, but that door was locked too. Then he ran down the steps to the basement entrance. He turned the handle and quietly slipped inside, shutting the door behind him.

"Anybody home?"

He still couldn't shake this uncomfortable feeling that something was wrong.

"Anybody home?" he called out again.

He walked up the basement stairs to the kitchen, and removed his boots and coat. He walked into the living room and looked around. At the bottom of the stairs to the second floor, he called out again. Still no reply.

So he went back into the kitchen. No one was around.

Then he noticed a note on the table. It was for Ravine.

Ravine, we have gone to Grandma's. We didn't want to wake you after your late night.

We'll be back by lunch. If you need anything, call Grace next door.

Love Mom and Dad.

Derek dropped the note and ran upstairs, yelling to Ravine. But no one answered him. He opened the door to her bedroom and flicked on the light. Her room was empty. She couldn't have! She shouldn't have tried to go through there again, especially not without him.

But he knew she did.

He looked in the mirror. The only reflection was his own.

Derek pushed against the glass. Nothing happened. He screamed for Ravine and started slamming his body against the smooth surface of what now seemed to be just a very ordinary mirror. He shook his head, confused and scared. He knew she was trapped.

Then, as he was about to try again, the mirror vanished.

Stunned, Derek dropped to his knees and began sobbing.

Ravine stood on the gravel path.

"Aren't you going to introduce me?" Henry asked again.

Abigail nodded and laced her arm through Ravine's. Ravine could feel the weight of Abigail against her. Ravine became dizzy with fright and she started to sway. But Abigail could sense that, and kept her steady.

"This is Ravine."

"I haven't seen ya around," Henry said gruffly.

"Oh, she's from a place down on Seven Mile Road. We met at the market a few weeks ago and we talked about her coming to visit."

"That's a pretty far distance from here," said Henry. "Who'd she come with? Where's her folks?"

Abigail said Ravine had ridden alone, and Henry seemed to accept that. At least he didn't ask where her horse was. He probably figured it was up at the barn.

Ravine was trembling beside Abigail, and she was surprised that Henry didn't seem to notice. He also didn't seem to notice that she was dressed only in her short nightgown.

He walked the girls to the house, and then disappeared into the barn to do chores for his Uncle Abe.

"I can't get back through the mirror," Ravine blurted out when they were alone. "I can't get back."

Abigail just stared at her. Ravine had never told Abigail that she appeared and disappeared through the bedroom mirror, and she wasn't sure if Abigail knew that.

Ravine was sobbing, and tears rolled down her face just as Meredith opened the door to find this unknown girl, hardly dressed, and crying.

"What's wrong?" Meredith asked. "Abigail, who is this girl?"

"Oh mama, this is my friend, Ravine. It's terrible. She was riding in the forest and she fell from her horse. It panicked and took off, and she couldn't find it. She's from way down past Seven Mile Road, and she has no way to get back home."

Meredith lifted the sleeping baby from the buggy, still staring at Ravine.

"Well, I am sure Abe can take her back home. It's alright, you'll be safe," she said to Ravine.

"But her house is locked, mama, and she doesn't have a key."

Meredith turned to Ravine. "That's strange. Why is your house locked?"

Ravine tried to calm herself. She was no good at lying, but she did the best she could.

"My ma and pa went on a trip early this morning to see my grandmother. That's my mama's mama. She's pretty sick, and they think she might be dying. We only have one small carriage, so there wasn't enough room for me. Papa didn't want me to come along beside them on our other horse, 'cuz it's a real big horse and I'm not allowed to ride it."

She paused, while Meredith fussed with the baby.

"But then I thought I would ride the horse anyway since no one was around to tell me not to. So I locked up the door and put the key in my pocket, where it would be safe. But when I fell off the horse, it spooked and ran away. When I got up, I couldn't find my key anywhere. I'm sure it must have dropped from my pocket some time while I was riding, 'cuz I couldn't find it where I fell."

Ravine started to sob even harder.

"Come inside," Meredith said. She put her arm around Ravine. "You can stay with us until we can get hold of your ma and pa."

Abe looked up as Meredith led the girls inside.

"Abe, heat some water. Abigail, go find some clean clothes for Ravine. You look to be about the same size."

Meredith gazed at the young girl in front of her. Her feet were bare and covered in dirt, and the dress was only thin cotton. It hung just past her bum. Meredith thought it looked sort of like a nightgown, except that it was far too short. This was not appropriate clothing for a young lady. She wondered what kind of family would permit a young girl to dress like this.

"We'll heat some water for your bath, and we can borrow you some of Abigail's clothes."

Ravine realized again that she was still wearing her short nightgown. She blushed.

After Ravine had soaked in a barrel full of hot water, Meredith placed some food on the table for the girls. They ate in silence as Meredith intensely watched the strange girl in front of her. Even Fredrick seemed interested in the new visitor. He continued to squirm in Abe's arms, but he was gazing at Ravine. And he was quiet.

After Ravine and Abigail climbed the ladder to bed, Meredith sat on the back porch rocking Fredrick. Abe sat beside her.

"I know all the houses on Seven Mile Road. This

girl does not live on Seven Mile Road," Meredith said, looking out into the horizon. The moon was just beginning to rise.

"I thought Abigail said she was from past Seven Mile," Abe replied.

Meredith rocked. Her gaze was still locked on the horizon.

"If she is from past Seven Mile, the closest line after that with houses is Eleven Mile. If that's where she's from, the girl is a long way from home."

Meredith thought a bit longer.

"I don't know where she's from," she continued. "But she's not from around here. I don't know where she comes from, but I am sure she is not from any county in these parts."

Meredith fell silent and continued to stare at the sunset.

"And did you see that flimsy dress she was wearing?"

Abigail and Ravine lay awake in the dark. The moon lit up shadows on the walls.

"How do I get home?" Ravine asked. They were sleeping in the same bed.

"I don't know," Abigail replied. "I thought you were just an imaginary friend. None of my other friends have come to life."

The girls stared at the ceiling.

"I wonder why you're here?" Abigail said out loud.

Ravine let that thought enter her mind. Her thoughts were getting increasingly blurry, and she seemed to be losing some of her memory. She found she couldn't quite picture Derek's face, although she knew who he was. But she had no idea why she was here, and even the thought that she had travelled through the mirror was starting to fade.

Her memories seemed to dangle at the tip of her brain, like when you are speaking but can't quite find the right word, even though you know it's right there on the end of your tongue. Ravine couldn't stretch out and grasp the memories. They were just a little bit beyond her reach.

She was from somewhere else, but where? She needed to do something in this world, but what? And where was her home?

"Yeah, I wonder why I'm here," she said before finally falling asleep.

Chapter 18

Ravine was wakened by the rays of the sun shining through the open window. She looked around trying to remember where she was. Then, when Abigail stirred beside her, she remembered the hot bath, the clothes that smelled of freshly picked daisies, and the last question that had entered her mind before she fell asleep.

Sitting up and stretching her arms above her head, Ravine arose and moved to the window. She stood there a few moments, letting the gentle breeze brush against her face, like soft lips tickling the tiny hairs on her skin.

"I'm scared, Abigail," Ravine said.

Birds chirped in the trees, and flitted back and forth around the barn. She recognized them as swallows, because she had seen them many times around the old house at 56 Water Street. Just at the edge of her line of sight, she could see Abe and Henry working out by the barn.

Abigail sat up in bed.

"Of what, Ravine? What are you afraid of?"

"That's just it. I don't remember. There is something I'm supposed to know, or I'm supposed to do. But I can't remember what it is. I only know it was really important."

Ravine sat back on the bed, and Abigail put her arm around her. The confusion in Ravine's mind was almost painful, and she felt more distressed than she could ever recall. The clearest thought she had had since she got here yesterday, was that Abigail would save her. At least she thought it was yesterday.

The room was silent, other than the cooing of two mourning doves that had perched on the windowsill. Then, a voice from below scared them off.

"Girls! Breakfast!"

Meredith called to them from the bottom of the ladder. Ravine could hear her opening the back door and calling to Abe and Henry. The girls dressed, and headed down quickly.

Abigail gave Ravine a light grey dress that hung just past her calves. She was surprised when Abigail gave her an apron to wear over it. Looking in the mirror she thought she looked like someone from a television show that she sometimes watched when she was younger. But she couldn't remember the name of the show, or the person she looked like. She knew it took place in some old cabin like this one.

Abigail got dressed beside her, in a similar outfit. Ravine thought about how mousy she looked beside this beautiful girl with the lovely champagne coloured hair.

Quickly, the smell of hotcakes and eggs floated up the ladder. Ravine realized she was famished.

"Coming, Mama!"

The table was set for five.

Abe and Henry let the door swing shut behind them as they entered. But at the last second, Henry remembered the sleeping baby and prevented the door from slamming. Abigail noticed this and smiled at him.

Abe gave Meredith a kiss on the cheek before sitting down, and said good morning to the girls.

"I'm a starvin' feller," said Henry. He started to help himself before anyone else had even taken a seat. Abigail sat directly across from him, and Henry quickly removed his cap.

"Mornin', Abby" he said shyly.

Abigail smiled at him again.

Breakfast was delicious, and Ravine took a second helping of everything.

"Mama, Ravine and I are going to saddle up Gent and go to the forest today. We want to try and find her horse, and maybe even her house key."

Abigail wasn't eating much, but she watched as Ravine was finishing up her third biscuit. Henry watched Ravine with amazement. He had never seen a girl eat so much food in one sitting.

"When your chores are done, then Henry can saddle up Gent for you," Meredith said. She and Abe were also watching Ravine with fascination. It was if the child hadn't eaten for days.

"I can help you with your chores, Abigail," Ravine said as she poured herself another drink. She didn't know what it was, but it was made from apples. It wasn't like apple juice, but it was good, whatever it was.

Ravine and Abigail cleaned up the kitchen and washed the dishes in a barrel that looked like a smaller version of the one Ravine had taken a bath in last night. When they were finished, they headed out and went around to the side of the house to fetch the laundry that had been airing overnight.

Abigail chatted endlessly as the girls folded sheets.

"Maybe you'll be here forever. Wouldn't that be great? I've never had a sister."

Ravine thought about it. Maybe it wouldn't be so bad. But there was something she was missing terribly; she just couldn't put her finger on it. There was something out there that gave her a sense of sorrow. Something she had lost. But couldn't remember what it was.

But when Abigail said she had never had a sister, something in Ravine's mind triggered and made her think that maybe she had one herself.

"Your mom is very nice. And Henry seems to like you a lot," Ravine replied.

Abigail turned to face her. She hugged the sheet against her dress.

"Oh, it's so strange," she started. "I never really liked him before, but then he gave me this beautiful necklace." She pulled it out from under her blouse to show Ravine, "And ever since then he has been so kind to me. I think I really like him."

Ravine noticed there was a second necklace around Abigail's neck, sparkling in the sunlight.

"Who gave you this one?" she asked pointing to it.

The locket hung on a delicate strand of gold. Abigail opened it up to show her the picture of a young gentleman.

"This is my papa. He gave me the locket when I was very little. After he died, my mama put his picture in it for me. I never take it off. It's very special."

By the time the girls were finished all their chores, lunch was ready. It was another big meal and Ravine ate as much as she could. Everything tasted so wonderful.

"Don't ride him too hard," Henry said, as he got Gent ready for his saddle. "I think he might have a bit of a sore leg."

"Don't worry, we won't."

Abigail patted Gent as Henry cinched the saddle. Ravine fed him some bits of apple.

"Okay, he's ready, Abby."

Abigail mounted first and then Henry helped Ravine up.

"I thought you said you knew how to ride a horse," Henry said. He shook his head. "You sure mount a horse funny."

Abigail looked behind her and Ravine blushed. She knew how to mount a horse, but not in a dress. She was more concerned about tucking the dress between her legs, not caring how pretty or capable she looked getting up.

Henry grabbed the reins and walked Gent to

the gravel path. He handed the reins to Abigail, reminding them one more time to be careful. Abigail smiled at Henry, then gently kicked the horse's flanks. He started off down the path toward the forest, gradually picking up speed as Abigail encouraged him. Ravine swayed from side to side, hanging on to Abigail for support.

Before they were out of earshot, Henry heard Ravine yell, "Not so fast, Abigail, I'm going to fall off!"

Henry headed back toward the barn mumbling to himself. There was something mighty different about that girl, he thought.

Derek paced. The mirror was gone. Ravine was gone. His heart was still pounding loudly against his chest. He had no way of reaching her. No way of knowing if she was alright, or even where she was. His head started to spin and he sat on the bed.

What if he never saw her again? His whole body ached. He put his head in his hands. Would she remember the other portal, the one he had come through when he fell from the cliff? Would it be open even if she did remember it?

Abigail and Ravine rode through the woods for what seemed like a long time. When the sun started to dip lower in the sky, it was obvious that they had been out for hours.

"We should be heading back," Ravine said. Her bum was sore. Her legs were sore. And she was hungry again. And this darn dress kept getting tangled up around her legs.

"Not yet," Abigail replied. "I want to show you something first."

Gent began to climb easily through the trees. Higher and higher. Ravine noticed his footing was soon laboured as he stumbled over lose rocks and tree roots, and he slowed down to a slow walk.

Then Ravine saw an opening, and noticed Abigail was steering Gent toward it. It wasn't long before they were looking down the face of a steep cliff.

Gent stumbled.

Ravine's heart pounded. She didn't like heights.

"Isn't this wonderful? You can see the whole world from here," Abigail exclaimed, as she steadied Gent who was still trying to get his footing.

"We're too close to the edge, Abigail," Ravine said. Her voice was shaking.

Gent stumbled again.

Ravine's heart pounded more loudly.

She looked down. The river rushed past far

below, and she could see large rocks jutting out of the rushing water.

Gent stumbled again, and Abigail held his reins tightly.

The sun was setting when Meredith stood on the back porch calling to Abigail. Abe and Henry appeared from the barn.

"Have you seen Abigail?" Meredith called.

"She came into the barn and asked to get Gent saddled after lunch," Henry replied, looking around. "She and that other girl took him for a ride."

"But it's dark. She should be back by now," Meredith said. Fredrick started to wail again just then, and Meredith rushed back inside to get him.

Gent stumbled again, even though Abigail held his reins tightly

Ravine's heart pounded even harder, and sweat tickled down the sides of her face.

"Let's get off and walk Gent," Ravine said. But Abigail seemed to be in a trance as she stared out over the valley.

Ravine's head began to hurt. Then, suddenly, she heard voices inside her head that got louder and louder. 'Get off the horse. Get off the horse. Get off the horse,' the voices said. It was a chorus of shrill voices. Louder and louder and louder. 'Get off the horse. Get off the horse. Get off the horse'.

"Aw, come on Meredith, please stop crying. You know how she gets distracted up in those woods. There's nothing up there to hurt her. She'll be along any minute now, you'll see."

"She's never been this late before, Abe, and it's dark."

"You know how she is, she'd forget her head if it wasn't attached. She probably lost track of time showing the forest to that new girl. She would have started to head back as soon as she realized it was getting dark. She'll be along any minute now, you just wait and see. "

"Abigail, we need to get off the horse. We need to walk Gent back down the path."

Ravine's voice was full of fear and panic. But Abigail sat frozen, her eyes glazed over, looking out to the horizon.

Gent stumbled again and kicked a few rocks over the edge. They disappeared down the cliff until Ravine heard the faint sound of splashing in the water down below.

"Please, Abigail," Ravine begged. Tears ran down her cheeks. "Please!"

Abe, Henry, and Meredith sat at the kitchen table. Meredith was cuddling the sleeping baby, while tears ran silently down her cheeks.

"Why don't I saddle up Lady, and see if I can't find her," said Abe.

"Oh, Abe, please go. I am awfully worried about the girl. She squeezed his hand as he patted her on the shoulder.

He pushed his chair back, scraping the floor, and walked to the door. His big black-laced boots echoed as he walked.

He pushed the back door open. "Don't you worry, Meredith, I'll find Abigail. Henry, you take care of everything here."

Henry nodded.

Gent stumbled again.

"Please, Abigail," Ravine begged.

Then Abigail seemed to come out of her trance, and she smiled.

"Okay," she said. "But there's nothing to be afraid of, really. Gent's been up here a hundred times. Abe says Gent is the most sure-footed horse he's ever seen."

Abigail swung her legs up and hopped down from Gent. Just as she was about to help Ravine down, the horse stumbled. He tried to regain his balance and his front legs flew up. He whinnied loudly in a fit of panic. Abigail tried to steady him with the reins, but he was a big strong horse. She stumbled backwards and the reins slipped from her hands. As Gent's hooves touched the ground, the rocks beneath him gave away he went tumbling over the side of the cliff, with Ravine still on his back.

Abigail screamed. She tried to grab the reins, but she was too late. She crawled to the edge. There was Gent laying on his side on the rocks below. Ravine had disappeared.

Abigail was still sitting alone, with her head in her hands and crying, when she heard the sound of hooves behind her.

"Abigail!"

She turned to see Abe leaping down from Lady and rushing toward her. He knelt down and Abigail flung her arms around him, sobbing uncontrollably.

"Oh, Abe! It's so awful," she gulped.

Abe patted her hair and rocked her back and forth trying to soothe her.

"Gent fell," she said, pointing behind her to the loose rocks at the edge of the cliff. Abe got up and peered down. There lay Gent, motionless. He turned back to Abigail and held her in his arms.

"It's all my fault," she sobbed uncontrollably. "If I hadn't been riding so close to the edge, none of this would have happened!" Her words rushed out as she gulped for air.

"It's okay, Abigail. It's okay." He held her close and tried to shush her tears away.

He took Abigail away from the edge of the cliff, and sat down with her on a big rock beside where he had tethered Lady.

"At least you are okay. At least it wasn't you who fell."

"But you don't understand. Ravine went over the edge with Gent. She's gone. I can't see her on the rocks, so she was probably carried away by the water. She's disappeared, and I'll never see her again. It's all my fault."

"Who's Ravine?" Abe asked quietly.

Abe and Abigail stared at each other.

"The girl who stayed with us last night," she said softly.

"No one stayed with us last night," said Abe. He paused and then said. "We'll get old Doc McLeod to come by the house tonight. You probably gave your head a good wallop."

Abigail looked back at the cliff, but Abe steered her away from it.

"Come on. I'll take you home."

Chapter 19

When Ravine looked up from the floor, she saw Derek sitting on her bed with his head in his hands.

"Everything is okay," she whispered.

Derek looked up, startled. There she was, sitting on the floor in front of him. He leaped off the bed and wrapped his arms around her, hugging her as hard as he could. She finally had to tell him to let go because she couldn't breathe.

"What happened? Are you okay? What happened?" He peppered her with questions as he released his grip on her.

"I know how Abigail died," Ravine said slowly. "She was riding her horse at the edge of the cliff. It stumbled over the cliff and took her along. It was the same cliff you went over.

"How do you know?" Derek asked.

"Because I was there. Only this time, instead of Abigail going over the edge, it was me."

They stared at each other. The portal that Derek had come back through was still open.

"You know what this means, right?" Ravine asked.

Derek nodded. It meant everything was okay now, she had made it back. He helped her up and led her toward the bed. She was cold and wet.

"I didn't think I would ever see you again."

Ravine tried to smile.

"We changed Abigail's fate. She was bucked off her horse a long time ago and fell off the side of the cliff. That's how she died. But she wasn't supposed to die then. It's like Isabel told me, not everybody dies when they're supposed to. And sometimes you can fix that."

She looked at the empty space where the mirror used to be.

"We helped her, Derek. We did what we were supposed to do."

Derek nodded. Instead of Abigail falling, it was Ravine. And luckily the portal at the cliff was still open. But maybe it wasn't luck. Maybe the angels that look after Ravine knew she was in Abigail's world, trying to help, and they made sure Ravine would get home safely. Now she was back where she was supposed to be. He had never felt such an emptiness.

"We need to go to the graveyard, just to be sure, though," she said. "I have to be sure."

"Okay," Derek said. "We'll go. But why don't you get cleaned up first."

Ravine shivered and stood up slowly. She wasn't surprised to see the mirror gone. That was a good sign. That was the way it was suppose to be.

Derek said he'd go and get some money to take a bus to the cemetery. There was too much snow on the ground for bicycles. And neither of them would have been up for that ride today anyway, even if the weather was good.

As he walked toward the door, Derek said, "Oh, and find some better clothes. You look like you just walked out of *Little House on the Prairie*."

Ravine looked down at her dress and smiled.

By the time Ravine was ready to go to the cemetery, her parents were back home. Snow was coming down hard now, so she was glad Derek had suggested taking the bus. He was already back with the money, and was waiting for her to finish cleaning up.

"How's grandma?" Ravine asked, following her parents into the kitchen. Derek followed behind.

"Well, her flu seems to be gone. But she's very weak still," her father said. They had stopped to pick up some lunch on the way home.

"Would you like to stay, Derek? There's more than enough. Linda, grab an extra plate," he said.

Derek sat down in Rachel's chair. He always felt uncomfortable sitting there. It just didn't seem right.

"Could you drive us to the cemetery after we eat?" Ravine suddenly asked, glancing sideways at Derek. She helped herself to a pile of French fries. After the wonderful food Meredith had cooked up, this didn't seem so special.

"The cemetery? Why on earth do you want to go there today?" asked her mother.

"It's almost Christmas, and I have been thinking about Rachel a lot."

Her mother nodded. Rachel died on Christmas day, so the holiday wasn't the same as it used to be for the Crawl family. It was as much a time for sadness, as it was for joy.

There were a few moments of awkward silence. Ravine thought about the Christmas tree her parents had set up in Rachel's hospital room. The two girls had spent hours making their own garlands out of Froot Loops.

"I'll drive you," her father said.

Derek and Ravine got out of the car, leaving her father behind.

"I'm just going to get a coffee," he said. "I'll be back in less than ten minutes, and then I'll wait right here for you."

Ravine slammed the door behind them, and she and Derek headed through the gates and up the hill.

They stopped briefly at Rachel's grave and Derek stood close to Ravine.

"I wonder what she'd look like now?" she said in almost a whisper.

Derek didn't know if she wanted him to answer, so he remained silent. But he figured Rachel would look exactly like Ravine. But maybe not quite as pretty.

After a few moments, they both said goodbye to Rachel and headed off to Abigail Baldwin's grave. It was a good hike from where Rachel was buried, and the paths had not been ploughed yet, so it took them some time to get there.

"It's not here."

They looked at a gravestone that used to be Abigail's. But now it read Geoffrey Jones, 1818-1824.

"Well, she has got to have died at some time. Or

she'd be more than a hundred years old by now," said Derek.

They walked further, reading inscriptions as they went. Ravine suddenly stopped.

"What's wrong?" Derek asked.

Ravine pointed, and Derek read the gravestone out loud.

"Abigail Adams, beloved wife of Henry Adams."

Derek looked at Ravine. He didn't understand, he said.

"Henry's last name was Adams. Abigail married Henry."

Suddenly Ravine felt something cold against her chest. She unzipped her jacket and pulled out a locket hanging on a delicate thread of gold as the wind rose up and blew fiercely all around them.

Ravine opened it.

There she was, with the champagne blonde hair, blue eyes, and innocent smile. Abigail Baldwin.

Chapter 20

The house was silent, and all the lights in the house were out, except Derek's desk lamp. He sat at his desk, fingering the envelope. Finally, he slit the top of it with a pair of scissors. He carefully unfolded the paper inside and took a deep breath.

Dear Derek:

It has been a few years since you answered any of my letters to you. I believe the last time you wrote to me you were seven years old. I still have that letter. I keep it folded up in my wallet. I know your mother didn't even help you write it because of all the spelling mistakes. After that letter, you never wrote again. I believe that was when I told you I would be getting married again and invited you and Danielle to the wedding. Your sister has never forgiven me. But I didn't think I would lose you too when I remarried.

Lots of things have happened in the past 4 years, and I would like you to come spend some time with me. London is a fantastic city, and I know you would really love it here. I was thinking it might be great to have you spend a whole school year over here. I've been talking to your mother about this and she also agrees this would be a wonderful opportunity for you.

I know Danielle is off to university next fall. I believe your mother said Danielle would be going to the University of Toronto. I am very proud of her. I'm proud of all my kids.

You'll be going into grade 7 next year, so it will be good time to come, because then you can graduate in grade 8 back home with all your friends. That is, if you choose not to stay here.

Please come. I'm sure you'll miss Summerhill, but I bet you'll really like it here as well.

Love Dad

Derek stared at the letter, rereading it several times. His fingers and mind went numb. He could hardly catch a breath. A whole year in England? A whole year without Ravine and his friends? And his mother? Even Danielle.

He picked up the letter, shut off the light and

headed downstairs. He needed some water, his mouth was dry, and he couldn't think clearly.

Derek flicked on the kitchen light, and was startled to see his mother sitting in the dark.

"Did you read the letter, Derek?"

LaVergne, TN USA
11 March 2010
175704LV00001B/13/P